Were Chronicles
Pack Alpha
Pack Enforcer
Pack Territory
Pack Rogue
Pack Community
Pack Mates

I0570416

Shifter Chronicles
Birds of Prey
Bear Claw
Eye of the Tiger
Coyote's Kiss
Wolf Pack
Lion's Claim

Bloodlines
Bite
Control
Embrace

What's Her Secret?
Designated Alpha

Bloodlines

EMBRACE

CRISSY SMITH

Embrace
ISBN # 978-1-78686-339-3
©Copyright Crissy Smith 2017
Cover Art by Posh Gosh ©Copyright December 2017
Interior text design by Claire Siemaszkiewicz
Totally Bound Publishing

EMBRACE

Dedication

This book is dedicated to my daughter — my world, my Comic Con partner and my biggest accomplishment, who's responsible for the throat punch scene. It was her idea and I had to add it in. Love you, baby. Thanks for always being there for your mama.

Chapter One

Kieran Smith hissed as the needle was pulled out of his arm.

"Don't be a baby," Dean Westbridge taunted without sympathy. He slapped a Band-Aid onto Kieran's wound with a smirk.

He growled at Dean, but his heart wasn't really in the threat. Six weeks after Kieran had found out that there might be something wrong with him, there were still no answers. He needed Dean in order to figure this shit out. The doctor who had tortured and experimented on him for ten years let it out that he'd added unknown concoctions to Kieran's DNA. Sure, Kieran had realized that he was stronger and faster than other Walkers, but he'd attributed it to his advanced agent training. Now, it turned out that he was an even bigger freak than he'd first thought.

"How're you feeling? Have you noticed anything out of the ordinary?" Dean questioned.

Kieran wished he could say for sure. Being a Day Walker already made him different from other

7

paranormals since there were very few of his kind. There weren't many others he knew to compare himself to. The Walkers that he did know didn't exactly like to talk about their abilities. In response to Dean's question, he shrugged.

Dean sighed. "I need you to tell me what's going on."

"I realize that," Kieran said. "I don't know the answer."

The human agent walked across the room to set the vials of blood he'd taken from Kieran and placed them in a bag. Kieran wouldn't consider Dean a friend but pretty close. Dean had been the partner of Dakota, Kieran's lover, for many years, so that connection held them together. Kieran made an attempt to get along with Dean for Dakota's sake.

"How're things going with Dakota?" Dean asked from the other side of the room.

Kieran stiffened. He couldn't help his reaction. "Why?"

"Jeez, Kieran," Dean complained. "I didn't mean anything by the question. I just wanted to make sure the two of you are okay. There's been a lot going on. You two moved into the new suite, right?"

"Sorry," Kieran muttered. It hadn't been an easy month and a half since they'd taken down the group responsible for the death, torture and kidnapping of both Walkers and shifters. Finding out that the same organization they worked for had high-powered agents involved had thrown them off their game. Trust, something that was hard for Kieran at normal time, was now nonexistent. Only his promise to Dakota had him coming to see Dean every week. If it wasn't for his lover's concern, Kieran would be staying far away from anyone who wasn't part of his inner circle.

"The new place is bigger, so Dakota likes it. I enjoy staying at the hotel to remain close to Alex. I guess it's just weird buying a suite with Dakota. Like I'm waiting for her to get tired of my bullshit and take off." His honesty surprised him. Kieran never talked about his feelings. Especially not with someone like Dean, who he didn't know all that well. He moaned. "Forget I said anything, please."

"Look, man," Dean said, "Dakota loves you. If you want to talk to me, I'm more than happy to listen. I want to help figure out what's going on for the both of you. Just give me time."

In response to Dean's words, Kieran nodded. It wasn't easy for him to rely on anyone except himself. He still held himself back from Remy, his wolf shifter partner, who he'd worked with since joining the Organization. He yanked down the sleeve of his black sweater before standing. He appreciated Dean letting him come down to his lab instead of him having to go into the medical wing. Kieran's past with medical experiments was only one of the many issues that he had to try to deal with. If he hadn't had the control of someone much older than he actually was, Kieran could have ended up being a danger to those around him.

Everyone around him was aware of the very thin line that Kieran walked.

Even his partner and lover knew that at any time, Kieran could fall off the straight and narrow. They loved him, anyway.

If it wasn't for the support of the small collection of friends, his family now, Kieran probably would have gone to the dark side years ago. But, luckily for the world, Kieran had motivation to remain sane and honest.

"Okay," Dean announced, drawing Kieran from his thoughts. "I'll send these off and see if there've been any changes."

"Thanks." Kieran shoved his hands into the pockets of his dark-washed jeans before strolling toward the door.

"Hey, K!"

Kieran paused, although he didn't turn.

"You're going to be okay. I'm going to make certain."

Without another word, Kieran left Dean's lab. He wasn't on shift tonight and he hated having time off. Now, he'd spend the evening thinking about Dean and his damn tests. Dean couldn't and shouldn't make promises that might be impossible to keep. Kieran needed a distraction. One of his favorite activities was messing with the other agents around, but, since he'd seen his boss's vehicle outside earlier, he knew better.

Caspar might give him more leeway than anyone else, but Kieran knew when not to press his luck. Having to deal with the higher-ups of the Organization as well as the Shifter Coalition running their own investigation was leading to Caspar being in a very bad mood. While Kieran might have liked to have taken his boss's mind off everything going on and provide some entertainment, he'd promised Dakota that he'd behave.

He was just about to reach the elevator when his cell rang. Kieran pulled the black device from his pocket and read the screen. Lettie, his former co-worker from his previous post, was calling. He still spoke to her when she decided he needed to know something, so she wouldn't be calling for no reason.

"What's up?" he asked in greeting.

"Your girl just called in for backup," Lettie said. "I don't like what I'm hearing."

Kieran stiffened. Lettie was the best fucking hacker in the world. He didn't know why she continued to monitor them even when she'd been assigned to a different office, but he was grateful. "Where is she?" he demanded.

"3412 North Washington, behind a closed electronic store. The original call was for a reported sighting of a wild animal. Wolf maybe," Lettie answered.

"And?" Kieran pressed. Dakota could handle a wolf shifter with no problem. A jaguar shifter, she was powerful, fast and smart. She was also highly trained.

"Neighbors are calling in more animal sounds and when Dakota radioed for backup, she was cut off," Lettie explained.

He didn't need to hear any more. Kieran went to the stairwell exit instead of waiting for the elevator. He ran down the steps two at a time. "Got it." He hung up, needing to concentrate on getting to his lover. There were times when he hated what she did for a living. But, unlike him, Dakota wouldn't ever be able to leave the Organization.

Centuries ago, a small group of Walkers, shifters and humans had decided to form an agency that would work in the shadows to keep the innocent and unaware humans from discovering the paranormal world. The entire Organization was staffed from the bloodlines of the original group. Because Dakota had been born the first child of a family involved, she'd been commissioned to service. She hadn't been given a choice. From a young age, she'd been aware that she wouldn't be raised or loved by her family. She only had one purpose — to become an agent.

As far as Kieran knew, he was the only active agent who didn't stem from the original families. Caspar had brought him in after Kieran had been rescued. Kieran often wondered why Caspar had enfolded him into the world of the Organization, but it didn't really matter. Kieran was an agent and he could make a choice to leave if he wanted. He wouldn't, though. There was no way he'd leave his partner or lover behind. He was in for life, because Dakota and Remy were. There was no retirement for Organization agents. They either died in the line of service or were employed until their usefulness ran out.

He slammed through the last barrier opening up into the underground parking lot then raced through the night toward his bike, intent on getting to Dakota. As was his habit, he'd parked his Harley down the street instead of in front of the building that housed their offices.

Kieran didn't bother with a helmet. He merely got his bike started and roared off. The area that Dakota had called from was across town. As she'd called for backup, another agent should be closer than him, but he didn't trust anyone else to have her back. She worked with a bear shifter and human, but Kieran was a Walker. The abilities and power that he offered was unmatched by any other agent. He was the only Walker in the Las Vegas division.

Swerving in and out of traffic, Kieran sped toward Dakota.

It was a good thing that he didn't have to be worried about being killed in an accident with the chances he took. The heavy Vegas traffic was always a hardship to get through, but at nine at night on a Friday, it was damn near impossible. This was the exact reason he rode his bike. He was able to fit through spaces and, yes, he might have used a couple of sidewalks, as well.

Flashing lights, chaos and screaming greeted him when he pulled into the parking lot of a boarded-up bar. He skidded his motorcycle to a stop, ignoring the human police officers trying to wave him away. It was obvious to Kieran that the humans would be no help in this situation.

"Sir! Get back on your bike and leave the area!" a young, freckled faced officer ordered.

Kieran had the urge to flash his fangs at the damn kid. Hell, he couldn't be older than twenty-one. This little twerp was absolutely no competition to Kieran. He resisted scaring the crap out of the officer. "I'm with her." He pointed toward Dakota.

"Oh, sure," the officer replied, paling a little.

Kieran held back a smirk. The young policeman no doubt thought he was some sort of shifter. But while the shifters of the world had come out to the public several years ago, letting their existence be known, Walkers were still kept secret. There was enough drama with humans knowing about shifters. Vampires, or whatever they wanted to name his species, would have the humans in a massive panic.

He stalked with care toward where Dakota was crouched peering in a hole inside the bar. Her two partners, Gabe and Dare, stood at her back, watching the crowds. While Dakota's attention was on whatever was happening inside, they had her six. Kieran approved.

"What's going on?" he asked, joining them.

"We think there's an injured shifter inside," Dare told him. "And a wolf and coyote shifter won't let us get close enough to get a good look, though."

Fuck, an injured shifter can cause a lot of damage if they panic.

"It's okay," Dakota was murmuring. "I know you're scared, but we're not here to hurt you."

She'd used that tone with him when Kieran was coming out of a nightmare or an episode of his past. He'd always found it comforting. Kieran hoped whoever she was speaking to picked up the honesty in her tone.

Kieran dropped to his knees behind her. "What do you need?" he whispered. He needed to stay out sight for now. If the shifters saw him, they'd pick up on his power and things could get a lot worse.

Dakota turned her head. "You're supposed to be off tonight."

He shrugged. There was no reason for her to be aware that Lettie monitored her calls when she was on duty. "I was in the neighborhood."

She scoffed. "I bet. We'll discuss this later. I sent the other agents to see if there was any other way inside. I don't want to force our way in if we can help it."

Yeah, the possible bloodshed involved wasn't good. Especially with humans close by.

"Just three inside?" he asked.

"That's all I can smell." She leaned back. "It's weird — they're really young. And how often do you see three different species together?"

"They've all shifted?"

"They are now. When we got here, just the bobcat and wolf were, but now the coyote has, as well. That's probably how they feel the safest."

"Sorry, Dakota." Two agents came from around the side of the building. "It's boarded up good. There's no way to get inside without ripping off some of the wood."

She shook her head. "That'd make too much noise. Send them into a panic."

"What do you want to do?" Kieran inquired. He could already tell that she was coming up with a plan.

"I can shift and go in."

"No." There was no question. He was not going to allow her to put herself in danger that way.

"K," she murmured. "We have to do this quick. There's no telling when a damn news crew will show up. I don't want these kids to be on camera. We need to get them out of here."

He glanced around and knew she was right. For the last several months, it had seemed that someone was tipping off reporters to every incident that they were investigating. That wasn't good when their Organization was meant to work in secret. Luckily, the news had associated them with the Shifter Coalition instead of realizing they were something much more dangerous. Already, a ton of people stood at the taped-off area where the local PD was holding them back. Numerous cell phones were being pointed at them as the humans took pictures and videos. He growled, still hating technology. When he'd first started working for the Organization, things had been so much simpler. He'd not had to worry about someone catching him and exposing his secrets. Now, the lives of the agents were put in jeopardy every time someone showed up to get their fifteen minutes of fame.

"I can go around the back and just punch my way inside," he said. "No one will even see me." Kieran would rather put himself in danger than her. What he was couldn't get out. The world was still stressing over the existence of shifters. If humans learned of vampire-type creatures, there'd be no peace for the paranormal community.

"Can't," Dakota said. "Caspar would kick both our asses if someone captured that."

He grunted. Like he gave a damn about what Caspar thought if it meant keeping Dakota safe. The more screen time she received, the less chance she'd be able to do her job. Dakota actually loved being with the Organization and protecting innocents while Kieran just didn't like to be bored. He found the excitement and danger worth the time he put in for work. Kieran wasn't a good person. He'd come to terms with his faults a long time ago. Dakota made him want to be a better man, but Kieran wasn't even sure that was possible.

"I'll shift. In my jaguar form, they should be more willing to follow me. I'm more dominant and their instincts will be to cower. I can handle this."

"Or they'll attack as soon as you get inside," he argued. "It'll be three against one."

"They're only kids, K."

God damn it, he didn't want her going in there alone, where he couldn't see or help. He also wasn't happy about her having to reveal her animal side in front of the public. "You." He pointed at one of the agents. "You got an SUV?"

"Yes, sir."

"Back it up to right here," Kieran ordered. "As close as you can get."

"Right away!" The male agent, human, hurried off.

"What are you doing?" Dakota gripped his wrist, frowning.

"You can transform inside. I don't want anyone seeing you. I'll open the back and you can jump from the vehicle to the building. If someone has the right angle, they might catch you, but it's the best we can do."

She nodded. "Good idea." Her features, which had been drawn and tight, softened. When she looked at him like that, Kieran felt like a king. Deep down, he knew eventually she'd stop when he disappointed her. For now, it was enough that she still believed in him.

"I'm staying right by the opening. I swear that if you get hurt, I will not be happy."

"I know." She lifted her hand to cup his cheek. "But remember that they're just scared kids."

He loved her. God, just looking at her concern-filled eyes, he lost his breath. After having had to live her entire life on her own, knowing she had no control about her future, Dakota was still the kindest person he'd ever met. The shifters inside were a threat. Dakota could choose to use force and capture them. Instead, she was revealing herself in order to help them.

She impressed the hell out of him.

It was probably his instincts, as well as past events of his life, which led him to want to use force to end the situation. Not that the kids inside would be harmed, but it'd take less time to force his way in and capture them. That made him feel shitty. Another reminder that he was truly a monster. He'd killed and he'd have to live with that. Sure, he'd only eliminated paranormals who had broken the law and hurt others, but he was tainted. Dakota lived her life for others. It was a small wonder what the hell she was doing with him.

"Be careful," he demanded.

"I always am." She rocked forward to press her lips against his.

Kieran grabbed the back of her head, forcing the quick peck she'd meant into a deep, meaningful kiss. Dakota opened for his probing tongue and her unique flavor burst onto his. He'd claim and mark her in any way that he could.

"The vehicle is coming," Dare said in obvious amusement. "Unless you want to go ahead and undress her here in front of everyone."

Kieran pulled away so he could glare at Dakota's partner. If humans hadn't been around, he would have flashed some fang.

Dare laughed. Kieran liked it better when everyone was terrified of him.

Dakota patted his knee before she stood. He followed suit. As Dakota moved off to the side, Kieran directed the agent in backing up. When the SUV was where he wanted it, Kieran opened the back door for Dakota.

"We're going to discuss you pushing into my call later," she warned him.

"Sure." Kieran would do it again. They both knew that.

"I mean it," she said. "You need a night off."

No, he didn't. Kieran needed to stay busy. The unease and twitchiness he'd always felt was stronger than ever. It was as though he could sense something big was going to happen. And when things happened to Kieran, they were always bad. He hoped all hell wasn't going to break out that night. Kieran was tired — exhausted, really. He could fight but hoped he wouldn't have to. "If I hear anything going wrong, I'll get inside."

With a roll of her eyes, Dakota climbed into the back seat. He slammed the door closed before motioning the other agents where he wanted them. He'd be the one closest to the opening. He wasn't kidding. If he thought she was in danger, he wouldn't care what he had to do to get to Dakota.

Inside the dark vehicle, Dakota was pulling off her shirt. Kieran walked to the back so he'd be able to open the hatch when she was ready.

As he waited, he looked around with a fierce look. A couple of the humans gawking started to shuffle where they stood. He was intimidating and he knew it. Kieran dared anyone to come close.

Dakota Reese had to take several deep breaths before she could start her transformation. She used to love to change into her jaguar form, but six weeks ago, she'd battled her powerful ex-boss and almost lost control. In the heat of the fight, Dakota's jaguar side had overpowered her human half.

No one other than Kieran knew about her fear of shifting. They'd been working on it together at home so that when she needed to transform in the field, she'd be able to. This was the first test. Dakota sent up a silent prayer that everything would go okay. She was secretly glad that Kieran had appeared, even if he should have been nowhere near a call since he wasn't working. Not that she was surprised he'd shown up. It had been happening a lot in the last few weeks. Whether he was on duty or not, Kieran had a habit of turning up where she was. It'd take some digging around, but she'd figure out how he was doing it. At least, thinking about him helped calm her and she felt the ease of the transformation roll though her.

Being a shifter was a marvelous and fantastic thing.

Dakota wasn't a scientist like Dean, so she didn't understand how her ability was possible. Some people were born with the ability to shift and some weren't. It all depended on their DNA. She loved the fact she could. *Or I did love it, until recently.* Her biggest fear was hurting an innocent and Dakota wouldn't be able to live with herself if that happened.

The transformation was quick and painless. One minute, she was kneeling as a human and the next she was seeing the world through different eyes. As a jaguar, her sight wasn't the sense that overpowered the others. Instead, scents bombarded her. Dakota picked up the odor of sweat, coffee and stale cigarettes from the other agents' vehicle.

She leapt over the back of the seat into the cargo area. As soon as she reached the back door, the hatch was opened. *Kieran.* Even in her animal form, she knew him. Her jaguar side loved him as much as she did when in human form. He was who she'd chosen as her mate. They never discussed mating or the future. It was enough for her to know that Kieran saw there was even a future between them.

"Hey, beautiful," Kieran greeted, rubbing her ears.

So much had changed in six weeks. A month and a half ago, he'd never seen her jaguar form and now he had no issues petting her. She ran her rough tongue around his fingers and he chuckled. When they'd first met, Kieran had hated every shifter but his partner Remy. There had been moments when she'd been afraid of him. Even as a shifter, she was no match for a Walker. Now, she had no doubt how much he loved her, even though he rarely said the words.

"Go ahead," he urged. "I've got your back."

She moved to the edge of the SUV and stared into the darkness of the boarded-up building. Inside, she could pick up the dark shapes of the wolf. That was the bravest of the teen shifters, but she still spotted his unease. They were afraid and, if she wasn't careful, they might hurt her by accident.

Dakota mewled at the other shifters, hoping the soft, gentle sound came out as comforting. She could only see one, but the others would be able to hear her. The fur on the wolf was raised in aggression. Damn, she needed the young shifters to remain calm. Kieran hadn't been joking when he'd promised to have her back. If Dakota was injured, he'd rip the building apart to get to her. She didn't want anyone hurt.

She repeated the noise while crawling out of the SUV and back to the opening of the building. There were nails sticking out of the boards and at least one of the shifters was bleeding. The aroma wafted up and her lips curled. She barely held back a snarl. The blood called to a deep primal instinct. Instead of giving into the hunter side, she concentrated on soothing the three scared teenagers.

The wolf growled and she grunted back in irritation. He had to know that she could easily take him down. She scooted forward until she was all the way inside the rundown bar. The dust and mold odor was strong. It was the heavier scent of blood inside that concerned her. The wolf snapped his jaws and she paused. There was a soft whimper farther back in the shadows. Where was the coyote? He had to be around there somewhere. With her belly to the ground, she studied the area, trying to see deeper into the dark. In the corner, she spotted the other two. A small coyote was crouched over the tiniest bobcat she'd ever seen. She kept the wolf in sight in the corner of her eye while lowering herself to try to appear less threatening. The coyote had his ears pinned back on top of his head, but the way his gaze darted around told her so much. Calmly she rose, the wolf stepped back, the coyote lowered himself and the bobcat whimpered. Making soothing noises, she carefully stepped closer and closer to the wounded bobcat. This was the moment that they'd attack if they were going to.

The wolf growled, but when Dakota turned her head and bared her fangs, he stopped. They were scared, but they wouldn't hurt her. She was certain now. Dakota nodded, trying to convey the sense that everything was going to be okay.

Reaching the wounded bobcat, Dakota ran her gaze over the trembling form. She rubbed her muzzle over the bobcat's uninjured side in comfort. The large gash had already started to heal, but it would take time and had to be painful. The ragged edge of the wound appeared to be from sort of weapon—it was obviously not a scrape from where he'd entered the building.

Dakota changed back to her human form, her movements quick. The two back to back shifts made her dizzy, but she ignored the feeling, concentrating on the kids instead. "Can you shift back? I need to know how to help you."

As the bobcat shook and whimpered, the two males exchanged glances.

"I just want to help," she said.

Dakota wasn't surprised when it was the wolf shifter who began to transform back to human. She hadn't gotten a good look at him before. He couldn't be older than fifteen or sixteen.

"Hi, my name is Dakota. What's yours?"

"Adam," he whispered. "Are you going to arrest us?"

"No. Can you tell me what happened?"

"You're not with the Coalition?" Adam asked instead of answering her question.

"No," she said carefully. The cynicism in his tone worried her. If they had issues trusting the police, her job had just gotten a whole lot harder.

"Human police?" Adam pushed.

"No."

Adam pressed his lips together but finally nodded. "We were jumped and Carmen got stabbed. I tried to get to her, but I was too late."

Dozens of questions popped into her mind, but the wariness in Adam's gaze cautioned her to choose her next words with care.

"I can take you somewhere safe," Dakota offered. "There's been too much attention drawn to this place, so you can't stay here." She peered around, noting that while the bar had been boarded up for a while, someone — her best guess was these three kids — had been living there.

"Just take care of Carmen," Adam said. "Jeremy and I will be fine."

"Not interested in a hot shower or free food?" Dakota hoped she could convince all of them back to headquarters. She didn't want to see them back on the streets.

"I don't want our stuff stolen," Adam replied.

Dakota sighed. While she might not understand what these kids have been through, she knew that they needed support. They were much too young to be on their own. "Take whatever you want. Hopefully, you won't have to come back."

"We're not going back to the group home," Adam argued. "No way."

"Okay," Dakota drew out. "I don't know what group home you're talking about, but if there's something going on — "

"We're shifters," Adam interrupted.

"And everyone else is human?" she guessed.

"Even the people in charge." Something flashed over Adam's face, but it was gone too fast for her to fully comprehend.

"You won't go back there," she agreed. Dakota knew better than to make promises she couldn't keep. If she broke her word, the kids would never trust her again. She'd figure out something else for the teens.

"That's what the agent from the Coalition said, too," Adam informed her. "He lied."

Dakota took a step forward and looked him in the eyes. "I'm not lying."

Adam stared back for several long minutes before he nodded. "You'll help Carmen?"

"We'll help all of you," she said. "Now, gather your stuff while I get Carmen to my partner."

"Go ahead and shift, J," Adam said to his friend.

The coyote pressed his forehead to Carmen's before stalking to Adam. Adam ran his fingers through his fur before patting him gently. The bond between these three was strong, making her wonder how they'd come together.

Dakota kneeled beside Carmen, the bobcat, running gentle hands over the animal's snout. Carmen stiffened but didn't try to move away. That was good. Dakota didn't want to cause her any more pain. "I'm going to lift you up and carry you to the door."

A yowl was her response, so Dakota took that as permission.

Carmen was light, too thin, and Dakota easily lifted her.

"Kieran," she called out.

"I heard everything," Kieran replied. "Just bring her here. I have a blanket in the back of the SUV to lay her on."

Of course, her lover had picked up every word. His hearing was better than anyone else's she'd ever met. She was halfway across the room when he started tearing out the rest of the boards to make a bigger hole.

By the time Dakota reached the opening, Kieran had his head inside, reaching out to take the small bundle in her arms. Dakota released Carmen into Kieran's hold, surprised when he bent his head, shushing the teen.

"Shh," Kieran whispered. "It's okay. We're going to take care of you. Just close your eyes and relax."

Dakota stared at him in shock. Kieran was a lot of things, but comforting and gentle was not one of them. Except with her. He was always kind and soft when it came to dealing with her.

"I'm going to get you the biggest, juiciest burger and salty fries." Kieran kept talking to the bobcat. "Ice cream for dessert."

Carmen whimpered.

Dakota turned when she felt the two boys at her side.

"Who's that?" Jeremy asked in awe.

"He works with me. He won't let anyone hurt your friend."

"I can feel his power," Adam said. Instead of being awestruck like Jeremy, Adam appeared frightened.

"He's a good man to have by your side," Dakota assured him.

Kieran laid Carmen into the back of the SUV before covering her up with a second blanket. He gave her a small scratch them motioned the boys forward. "Climb in the back. Let's get you going. The news van just pulled up."

Adam and Jeremy scurried to comply as Kieran grabbed Dakota's clothes and tossed them at her.

"Thanks." Dakota dressed quickly, not wanting to let the teens out of her sight for long. She listed to the side when she got one leg into her jeans, but Kieran was there with a hand on her elbow.

"You okay?"

"Yeah, fine," she answered. "Haven't shifted so close together in a while."

"And you didn't eat dinner," he commented.

Dakota rolled her eyes and Kieran frowned.

"You never know when you're going to transform while on shift," Kieran chided. "You need to make sure you eat."

"I'm fine." She didn't need Kieran going into mother-hen mode. It was bad enough that Dean nagged her nonstop over eating. She didn't need Kieran's shit, too. "I am a grown woman."

"Who takes care of everyone but herself?"

"K." She grabbed the hem of his shirt and pulled him forward. "How many times do I have to tell you that I can take care of myself?"

"You don't have to," Kieran disagreed. "You have me now. And I will make sure you eat, and sleep and whatever else I feel like you need."

As annoyed as she'd been growing Kieran managed to touch her heart with his gruff words. "I'll get something as soon as I get the kids settled."

Kieran grunted. "Gabe switched vehicles with the other agents, so the two of you will drive the teens in while the others wrap things up here. I'll be right behind you."

"Okay." She leaned up against him. Kieran wasn't this gentle with anyone other than her. Not even with his partner Remy. Instead of getting irritated, she softened. "I appreciate that you care. But I need to be able to do my job here."

"I'm helping," he insisted. If Kieran got his way, which unfortunately he usually did, he'd do whatever he wanted. Each set of agents were given assignments, patrol areas. Kieran showed up wherever he wanted, though. Dispatch hated having him on roll.

Dakota shook her head. "Isn't there a poker game that Alex is trying to get you involved in?" Maybe using Kieran's oldest friend would help get Kieran's mind off her. Kieran didn't enjoy life enough. It was Dakota's mission to make him smile more.

"He's still teaching me," Kieran said. "He says I have the best poker face he's ever seen, but I can't keep growling at the competition."

She laughed. God, she loved her man. It was just like Kieran to intimate his opposition, even in something as simple as a game. "Go! I'm heading in."

"I'll follow you."

"Kieran," Dakota said. "I'm just going back to the office. By the time I get the kids settled, I'll be off."

"You're going to need help. It's not like I made other plans." He turned and stalked off toward his motorcycle.

Shit, his jeans hugged his tight ass to perfection. She wondered how often he caused accidents by distracting other drivers. Dakota rolled her eyes. *Okay, time to get to work.* She could fantasize about Kieran later.

Hell, she didn't even have to fantasize. Dakota got to put her hands on Kieran whenever she wanted. More so. In her past relationships, Dakota had had more of a friends-with-benefits arrangements. She hadn't expected the intense connection between her and Kieran. Dakota wouldn't be able to return to the way she used to live—Kieran had ruined her for anyone else. He liked it that way. If she was being honest, Dakota did, too.

Chapter Two

Kieran stopped by the closest fast food restaurant, picking up enough substance for Dakota and the teens. Sure, their office had a nutrition bar-cafeteria, but that food wasn't what the shifters needed right now. Kieran knew how to take care of his lover and her new charges.

He stashed the food inside his backpack before pulling out onto the street.

As he swerved in and out of traffic, Kieran thought about what could be done with the three teens. They needed somewhere safe to stay and, from what he'd overheard earlier, the kids weren't going to make it easy for them. It was lucky that Kieran had more money than he'd ever be able to spend.

Money had actually never been an issue. He hardly spent what he received from the Organization. On top of his salary, Kieran had family money. What he considered blood money, in every way. Shaking off those disturbing thoughts, Kieran needed to concentrate on the future, not the past. Instead of parking down the street as he preferred, Kieran drove up to the guardhouse, instead.

"Agent Kieran," the man greeted. "Go ahead."

Kieran didn't have time to screw with the agent or he would have. Messing with the guards was one of his favorite activities, after all. He pulled into a spot right next to the SUV Dakota had driven. Her scent was still fresh, meaning he wasn't too far behind. Hurrying to catch up with her, Kieran followed her delicious aroma up the back stairs. As he suspected, she'd taken the teens straight to the medical wing.

Ignoring the agents he passed, Kieran strolled down the hall. Before he could enter the room Dakota had gone through, he heard yelling.

"Don't touch her!"

"Adam! Dean is only trying to help," Dakota said quietly and steadily.

Kieran pushed the door open. The scene was a mess. Both male teens were covering the tiny scared female. Dean stood next to the window, holding up his hands in a *calm down* gesture as Dakota stood next to the bed.

Adam growled at Dakota. Kieran let the door slam closed behind him.

Everyone turned to him and Kieran raised an eyebrow. "What's going on here?" he asked, his voice mild.

"It's okay," Dakota said. "Everyone just remain calm."

Kieran sauntered from the door to the rolling table tray. "I brought food. Good food." He began pulling the bags from his backpack. The scent of burgers and fries filled the small room and Kieran was glad to see he had the three kids' attention. "I got plenty for everyone."

"Kieran," Dakota murmured.

"No," Kieran said. "These kids need food. Then they can be poked and prodded."

"I'm all for that," Adam agreed. He was still eyeing Dean with suspicion.

Jeremy was nodding enthusiastically.

Dakota sighed.

"Did you get enough for me, too?" Dean asked.

"Yep." Kieran held up a wrapped sandwich in each hand. "Burger?"

"Please." Dean caught the package.

Adam and Jeremy sat next to Carmen. Luckily, the beds were made for extra-large shifters and the three of them could all lean against the pillows. Kieran smiled at them while passing out three burgers and large fries for each of them. Kieran then passed the food to Dakota. "Everybody needs to fuel up."

"I don't even know how you can surprise me anymore," Dakota whispered. She started digging into to the fries. "But you do."

Kieran waited until she'd shoved several in her mouth before taking some for himself. "I like to keep you on your toes. Besides, I told you that you needed to eat."

"I know." She grinned at him.

For several minutes, the only sound that could be heard was chewing and groaning in delight. Kieran took the opportunity to get his first good long look at the three teens. They were scared, that much was obvious, but they also had an inner strength.

It was no secret how much he despised shifters, but he couldn't pull up any of those old feelings. Instead, Kieran felt some kind of kinship to them.

For years, he'd had no control over his life and what had been done to him. Away from home for the first time, with no one to guide him, Kieran had fallen into the crutches of evil men at eighteen. He couldn't let the same thing happen to these youths. Damn, he could already feel the bonds tethering them together.

He almost left right then.

Didn't he have enough complications in his life? Kieran was up to his eyeballs in problems and now he was considering adding in three children, who he didn't even know? Yes, he was. He noted Carmen had started to drift off, with her food still in her lap. Fuck, yes, he was.

"Thank you for the food," Adam said.

Kieran nodded. "Now, you have to let Dean check you three out."

Adam eyed Dean warily.

"Hey." Kieran walked up to the side of the bed to stand beside Dakota. "I know you don't trust us. But Dean's an okay guy."

"Jeez, thanks," Dean deadpanned.

Kieran winked at him.

"What are you going to do?" Jeremy whispered.

"Nothing that will hurt," Dakota assured him. She glanced at Dean for confirmation.

"It won't," Dean agreed. "First, I'd like to examine Carmen. She should be healing, but I don't want her to get an infection or anything."

"I can stay with you the whole time," Dakota assured the girl.

"Why don't I show the boys where they can shower?" Kieran offered. Getting them out of the room seemed like the best scenario. They were overprotective of the small girl. Plus, Dakota was going to start asking questions soon. The teen boys didn't need to hear the answers. Part of the examination included making sure no one had sexually abused the poor young lady.

"Good idea," Dean said. "We'll probably only need ten minutes or so. If Carmen wants, I might give her something to help her sleep."

"Where are we going to be?" Jeremy asked. "She shouldn't be alone."

"I figured the three of you fitted in the bed just fine earlier," Dakota said. "I can have some cots brought in, if you prefer."

Adam and Jeremy looked over at Carmen.

She discreetly patted the bed.

"We're fine. Just don't try to separate us," Adam warned.

"I wouldn't dream of it," Dakota responded. She nodded to Kieran.

"Let's go." Kieran motioned for the boys to follow him. Both appeared uncertain, but it was Carmen who motioned them away.

Adam glanced back at Carmen, though.

"I'll be fine," Carmen said. She peered up at Dakota. "I trust them."

"Fine." Adam rose from the bed, his movements reluctant. "But we'll be right back." He said it like a warning. That was actually kind of funny. Kieran was one of the most powerful beings in the world and this child was threatening him? *Yep, funny.*

"Come on," Kieran ordered. He walked to the door, knowing the boys would follow him. They'd be curious enough for now. Hopefully by the time he got them cleaned up, he'd have some kind of plan.

Dakota was going to trust the Organization to help the teens, but Kieran still had issues with letting anyone else control things. Between his money and connections, Kieran just needed to choose the path he used.

Instead of taking the elevator, he went directly to the stairwell. The boys were in pretty good shape, especially with the recent meal, and didn't complain. They also didn't talk, not to him or each other. Still, Kieran felt the bond was strong between them.

He led them to the men's showers. No one else was inside, which Kieran was grateful for. Not that he'd come across trouble, but the agents were nosy. Kieran stomped to his locker and used his key to undo the lock before pulling open the metal door. He grabbed his toiletry bag and tossed it to Adam.

Adam caught the mesh bag easily before glancing down at it.

"Go ahead and shower. I'll find you both some clean clothes," Kieran said.

Adam glanced toward the open tiled shower area. Jeremy was practically bouncing on his toes. Kieran had the feeling it'd been a while since they'd gotten a good shower. He knew how it felt to be dirty and street-worn.

"Take your time," Kieran suggested. "Dean can wait to look you two over." He hoped the boys would take advantage.

"Thanks." Adam passed the bag to Jeremy and nodded for the coyote shifter to go. Jeremy didn't waste any time. He rushed forward and had one of the showerheads on in an instant.

Kieran waited, since Adam didn't follow his friend. "What's on your mind?" Kieran asked.

"I'm wondering what you and your girlfriend get out of helping us."

"Maybe we're just good people?" Kieran quipped.

Adam snorted.

"Okay." Kieran waved his hand. "Dakota is a good person and she really does want to help just because she can."

"And you?"

Kieran sat on one of the long benches and motioned for Adam to join him. "I've been in your shoes. Neither of us see the good in the world. We know it can be hard and there are monsters out to get us."

Adam nodded slowly.

"I've been powerless. It's not something I ever want to feel again. I think I see a kindred spirit in you. Your friends trust you because you'll die to protect them."

"You saw that in seconds?" Adam sounded skeptic.

"I'm good at reading people."

At least he got a smirk from the wolf shifter. "What are you?"

Kieran shook his head. Even some paranormals didn't know about his kind. The ones who did feared Kieran. "Another time. For now, take your shower."

"Fine." Adam rose and followed Jeremy. Kieran watched the young shifter go.

It felt strange to Kieran that he had all these feelings bubbling up inside him. He blamed Caspar for making him come here, Remy for being the first person he connected with and Dakota for making him fall in love for the first time in his life. It would be so easy to just walk out of the door and never look back. He didn't have to watch his back any longer. The shifters who had tortured him were gone. He had money and connections. If Kieran wanted to, he could disappear.

Kieran lifted his head and glanced toward the two young shifters.

No, he would be walking away from his life.

Dakota was the person he'd spend the rest of his life with. Even though it was still hard to admit just how much he loved her, Kieran hoped his actions spoke for him. He might not ever deserve her, but no one else would love Dakota like he did.

And this was fucking ridiculous. He didn't ponder his thoughts and feelings. With a growl, Kieran stood. He needed to get the boys some clothes and thought about the agents he worked with. After walking over to one of the lockers across from his, he wrenched open the door, busting the lock in the process. He grabbed what smelled like clean clothes from a gym bag and yanked them out. They should fit Adam and Jeremy and give him the chance to fuck with one of the humans. That thought made him grin. If Kieran didn't screw with someone at least a couple times a week, people might think he was going soft.

It took hours, but Dakota finally had all three shifters in a large room sound asleep. They'd all passed the medical evaluations and would physically be just fine. She wasn't certain about emotionally, though. They seemed to have formed a tight bond, which worried her. Shifters weren't known for embracing different species.

Adam would be the easiest to place. Dakota had worked with the Alpha of the local Pack before and knew Damon would be able to help a lost wolf shifter. Felines were more solitary creatures than wolves, but there were a couple of big cat organizations that helped transition feline shifters into productive members of society. Jeremy, the coyote shifter, would be the hardest to find a home for. Coyote shifters lived in Packs, but they didn't normally accept another outside their family. The bloodline was very important to the coyotes and, if Jeremy didn't have family, he might always be alone. She needed to think more on what to do for him.

She'd ask Kieran his thoughts, but her wayward mate had disappeared. Shit, she had to stop thinking of Kieran like that. They might be living together and in love, but no way was Kieran ready to discuss mating. She didn't know if he'd ever be.

Dakota struggled with the need to claim him. Her jaguar wanted to mark her man so that all others were aware he was taken. After what Kieran had been through at the hands of other shifters, Dakota had doubts on how much further their relationship could go.

Stop thinking about it, she scolded herself. Ever since they'd moved into a permanent suite in the hotel that Kieran's best friend Jackson owned, she'd been feeling like something big was right around the corner. Dakota just wasn't sure what. Hadn't they been through enough? When would things settle down and give them a chance to just relax and live their lives? She pushed open the door, exiting out into the parking garage. She stopped, spotting Kieran leaning against his bike. "Hey," she called. "I thought you'd left."

Kieran stood. "I was waiting on you."

"You're not even on shift and yet you spent the entire night here," she complained. It wasn't that she minded really, but Kieran needed to spend some time away from the Organization.

"You were here," he stated.

Comments like that were what kept Dakota hoping for more from him eventually. Kieran was trying to give her what she needed. If she wasn't certain about where they were going, she at least knew where they were right then.

"Did you feed?" she asked in a whisper. When left on his own, Kieran didn't take blood the way he needed. He hated having to rely on the blood.

"I will."

"Kieran." She wrapped her arms around his neck. "You have to take care of yourself."

"I'd rather take care of you."

The way he ran his hands down her back to cup her butt and lift her was familiar. If Dakota let herself, she'd get lost in his embrace. It wouldn't matter that they were in a public space where one of the other agents could come across them at any time. "Kieran…"

"Just one taste," he purred against her lips. "Please."

Like she'd ever turn down that request. "Just one."

Dakota lowered her mouth to seal her lips to his. The spark was instant. A zip of electric current that ran between their bond. She still didn't know if that was unique to them or how it worked.

Closing her eyes, Dakota gave in to the feel of her mate. Kieran ran his tongue over hers in a sort of dance. This wasn't just a simple kiss. Instead, Kieran devoured her. She lost everything except for him. Tightening her arms and legs around him, she started to hump against him. His hard erection was trapped between them and he groaned.

"Shit!" he said when he pulled his mouth away.

"I told you we shouldn't do this here," she panted.

"Get on." He nodded toward his bike. "I want to take you for a ride."

She gave him a wicked grin. "Oh, I like taking a ride on you."

Kieran snorted. "You bad girl." He slapped her ass before he let her legs go so she could drop her feet to the ground.

Dakota ignored the warmth in her butt from his hand as she climbed onto his motorcycle behind him. It'd been a while since they'd taken a ride together. She wrapped her arms around his stomach, burying her hands under his leather jacket. Pressing her face to his back, she took in the heady scent of leather. Scent was important to shifters. It was how shifters could tell friend from foe and what was going on around them.

Walkers didn't have a scent, though. Everyone else at least picked up odors from their surroundings. Whether it be what they ate, where they walked or a natural aroma. Kieran didn't smell like anything. It was the lack of scent that let her know what he was.

Kieran started his bike and revved it up a few times before taking off. She held on tight as he drove out of the parking lot and onto the street. Instead of taking the back streets that led to the hotel, Kieran turned toward the bright lights of the Strip.

Usually Kieran stayed away from the crowds and tourists. He didn't like people at normal times and of late had been avoiding them at all costs. Their new suite even came with a secured elevator that wasn't available to the rest of the hotel guests. It only had access to a few of the higher floors that the owner Jackson used and the suite he'd sold to them. Entering by a side locked door, Kieran no longer needed to enter the hotel by the main entrance.

"Where are we going?" she asked. With his superior hearing, he'd have no trouble catching her words.

"You'll see."

She sighed but settled in for the ride. Unlike Kieran, she enjoyed driving down the busy street at night. The mix of humans interested her. They were why she worked for the Organization. Each human that came to town, spent a little or lot of money then returned home safely never knew about the monsters in the shadows. That meant she'd done her job.

For centuries, her family and the other bloodlines who ran the Organization had stayed hidden. They still were. Even though the shifters had announced their presence to the world, the Organization remained secret. The world had the Shifter Coalition that policed the shifters and looked out for them. They didn't need to know about the Organization or other paranormals that hadn't been revealed.

She didn't mind working in the shadows for the most part. Dakota didn't need recognition or acclaim. Just knowing that she was making a difference was enough. It wasn't like she had another choice, anyway. She'd been born for one purpose — to serve.

The firstborn of every generation was required by blood oath to join the Organization. From the moment she'd been conceived, her parents had known that she would be leaving. That was why they hadn't loved her or shown her the same kind of affection that her siblings had received. Dakota needed to believe that, anyway. The Reese family had given her away to the Organization without a second thought. Dakota tried not to think about them often. She'd seen the way that Kieran's partner Remy's Pack and parents still loved him. Remy went home often and remained part of the Pack. Instead of turning their backs on their firstborn like Dakota's family, Remy's still kept constant contact.

Biting her lip, Dakota shook away her thoughts.

It didn't matter what her family did or didn't do. She was making one of her own. She had Dean, Gabe and Dare. They'd had her back since she'd joined the Organization. She'd gotten closer to Remy since his and Kieran's transfer. Then there was her lover and the Walkers that came with him. They might be an unusual group, but they were strong and kind. They were hers.

She squeezed Kieran's waist.

"You okay?" he called back.

"Perfect," she replied. Dakota needed to stop worrying about the future and enjoy her life as it was.

Kieran continued to drive them away from the city center and she knew where he was headed. They didn't go often, but she was familiar with the area.

Another thirty minutes and he pulled the motorcycle up to the entrance of the park. This was the designated area where shifters were able to transform. Humans were not allowed there at any time. Even though in their animal forms they kept their human intelligence, instinct was still strong. There hadn't been any shifter attack on humans.

Kieran turned off the bike and the quiet of the night was sudden.

"I already shifted," she said. "Why are we here?"

"Because you need to enjoy your jaguar form again. Not just bring her out to do your job."

She knew he was right. With her fear of being able to control herself, she hadn't been enjoying changing.

"I want to spend time with you. Maybe run a little."

Dakota grinned. Kieran could actually keep up with her. "I think I'd like that."

"Good." Kieran helped her off the back of the bike. "Let's do this."

She found a spot under a large oak tree that would be perfect to leave her clothes. While Kieran secured his bike, she began to undress. Once naked, she turned toward him to see that he was watching her closely.

"Ready?" she asked.

Kieran yanked his shirt over his head. He'd already draped his jacket across the seat of the bike.

Damn, he's fucking hot!

He stood with his chest bare, in jeans and boots. Dakota was hungry for more than just dinner. She wanted Kieran badly. But first she needed to give in to her jaguar.

Dakota dropped down to her hands and knees, which made transforming easier. Closing her eyes, she pictured her jaguar in her mind. The change came over her instantly. In just moments, her body began to shift.

With her head back, she roared. The sound echoed around the trees and open space. It felt good to be able to announce her presence. Warn away anyone else who might be in the area. Sometimes she didn't mind having company, but tonight she wanted it to be only her and Kieran.

Stalking forward, she kept her gaze on her mate. In this form, the need to mark and claim was even stronger. Dakota ignored the instinct to climb on top of Kieran and rub her scent all over him. It wouldn't work, anyway. He couldn't hold her aroma.

"Hey, baby." Kieran dropped to his knees, holding out his hands.

Dakota walked right up to him so that her weight knocked him back on his ass. Kieran chuckled but wrapped an arm around her middle before burying his face in her fur. With a rumble, she let him know how much she liked his hold.

"You are so beautiful," he said.

She loved the way he spoke to her, even though she couldn't talk back.

"Your fur is so silky and soft," Kieran murmured. He rubbed his big hand down her flank. "Are you ready to run?"

Dakota turned her head and licked up his cheek.

Kieran sputtered before pushing her away. "Stop that."

She danced back a few paces before coming right back up to him and nipping at his pants.

"Oh, I see how it is," Kieran bitched as he stood. "You think you're funny."

Making a circle, she darted in and out.

Kieran flashed his fangs. "I bite back, baby."

She purred at the sight of his sharp teeth. Dakota didn't have a problem with him taking her blood, but Kieran always refused to feed from her. It made her slightly nauseous and Kieran hated making her sick. Still she wished that he would take the substance he needed from her.

"You want a head start?" he teased.

She yowled then shook her entire body.

"Let's go." Kieran raced off using his Walker speed.

Dakota growled and leapt after him. The hunt was on.

Since she couldn't follow his scent, Dakota had to rely on the forest around her. Sounds echoed, bouncing off boulders, but she could also pick up his faint steps. She darted around a tree, thinking he'd be there. Just as she pounced, he put on another burst of speed and took off. *Fuck, this is fun.*

There was a small creek close by. After a good fifteen minutes of playing, she noticed Kieran leading her in that direction. Dakota loved water. She didn't care if it was a stream, creek or the bath. In her jaguar form, she always had so much fun playing.

The freshness of the water caught on the wind and she stopped following Kieran, instead sprinting to the stream. She didn't even pause. Once she reached the rocky bank, Dakota leapt as far as she could. She landed several feet away.

Kieran's laugh was soft until she ducked her head under.

Using her powerful tail and back legs, Dakota made circles while splashing around. Normally big cats didn't like the water, but for some reason, jaguars were different. Dakota enjoyed the water even more than any other jaguar, though.

It was just freeing to be weightless and powerful.

Popping up, Dakota gazed into the dark to see Kieran sitting on the bank, watching her. She turned and used her tail to spray water toward him. He didn't even move.

Chuffing, she went back to dipping her head down.

It probably took about thirty minutes for the fatigue to start to set in. She wasn't cold with her thick fur, but her muscles were tired and she'd begun to exhaust herself. Even though she'd have loved to stay longer, she started to paddle back to her mate. It was slow going, but finally she reached to edge of the water and walked out. With a huge shake of her body, she sent water in all directions. Kieran cringed but still remained sitting.

The cool wind ruffled the hair on her back.

"Come here, baby."

Like she wanted to go anywhere else. Dakota stalked forward until she was in Kieran's personal space. He pulled her down into his lap. With his big hand holding her down, she cuddled into him.

"I like it here," he murmured. She laid her head on his lap looking up at him. "It's so quiet."

She purred when he started to scratch under her chin.

"We should come out here more often. I know that you like it and I had fun. Maybe we could even get Remy to join us."

Dakota hated not being able to talk to Kieran. She started her transformation. Kieran didn't move away. She lay against him, panting and sweating.

"You didn't need to shift back," he said.

"I wanted to talk to you."

Kieran lowered his head and kissed her. Dakota opened up, allowing him to slip his tongue inside. Since she was naked already and he was only half-dressed, she hoped she could talk him into a little more than a kiss.

Raising to her knees, she pushed him back.

He laughed. "This isn't the most comfortable place for this."

"You should have thought about that before you were sitting here all sexy."

"Sexy, huh?" He preened.

"You know it," she confirmed. "Now you're mine." It didn't take more than a few seconds to get his fly down and have his cock out in the open. He was already hard and wanting.

Dakota dipped her head and licked at the crown of his shaft.

Kieran groaned as he slid his hands though her wet hair.

"Tastes so good," she hummed.

"Suck me." He lifted his lips as he spoke.

Without another word, Dakota took his cock into her mouth and swallowed. He began pumping up and she allowed it. The feel of his shaft over her tongue totally turned her on. The bursts of precum she got made her hungry for more. Using every trick she knew, Dakota put all her energy into giving him head. Kieran ran his fingers over her ass and she spread her legs wider so he could reach her wet pussy.

Dakota wanted him inside her. Whether his fingers or cock, she didn't care.

He slipped a finger inside as she continued to bob her head. It didn't take long for him to start shaking and Dakota herself needing more. Pulling off his hard-on, Dakota gazed up at Kieran.

"I want to ride you."

"Yes," he hissed, already helping to move her into position.

Hovering over his cock, she grasped the base and lowered herself down slowly. Dakota dropped her head back as he filled her. His flesh was stiff and slick pushing inside her. She barely let him all the way in before raising up then slamming back down. Kieran gripped her hips hard.

They moved together in a fast rhythm, edging them both closer to climax. Dakota opened her eyes and stared up at the moonlit evening as she used Kieran to get off. Above them, the canopy of leaves gave away enough for her to make out the nearly full moon. There was magic in the way nature accepted them. The two of them just fitted and the natural scents of the foliage only added to her arousal.

Dakota was a goddess here, while in reality, she was normal. But under the night sky with Kieran worshipping her body, Dakota was a goddess.

"Harder," she demanded. "I want to feel you deep." Even though she'd asked for it, Dakota wasn't prepared for Kieran to flip her back and plunge at supernatural speed. She cried out, screaming his name in ecstasy.

"Like this?" he panted. "This what you want?"

She scored his back with his nails. "Yes!" she hissed.

"Then take it! Take all of me!"

Her entire body was shaking with the force of his thrusts. A human lover had never been able to give her this intense, consuming lovemaking. Only Kieran could make her body sing this way. Leaves stuck to her back and to her hair. The sweat that slicked their bodies made their glide smooth. She had to yank away to breathe.

"Please!" she begged.

Kieran slid his hands under her ass, lifting her. The new angle had Kieran plowing deeper. There'd be no bruises from the desperate thrusts. Or his tight hold. Fuck, she loved being a shifter. Kieran knew she wouldn't break. He didn't have to hold back so she encouraged the frantic pace.

Her vision actually dimmed as her orgasm was ripped from her.

"That's what I want to see," he panted. "You giving in to me."

"Always," she managed.

"Because you're mine." Kieran ground his hips then paused. He towered over her, his pale flesh glowing. Sweat dropped from his forehead to her shoulder. Dakota was shocked she didn't hear a sizzling. They were fucking hot together.

"Yes."

"Yes," he repeated.

"All yours."

Kieran continued to pump. Now that she could think again, Dakota was able to stare up into his eyes. The bright blue she only saw when he was feeding or this heavily aroused.

He grunted as his arms shook from bearing his weight.

Dakota could practically taste his need on the tip of her tongue. "Give it to me," she ordered.

"Uhh," he managed, plunging fast again. Then he closed his eyes and released.

Chapter Three

Kieran was pretty sure that he and Dakota made a picture, stumbling in the side door to the hotel. They were both rumpled and dirt-covered. He led her toward the private elevator, almost bumping into Jackson Wickham.

Jackson was the only person in the world who understood Kieran's past. Kieran knew that they'd always be connected because of the hell they'd lived through. Other than Remy, Jackson was his best friend. Kieran leaned on Jackson more than he should. He lived in the man's hotel. Used his resources when needed. And looked to the older Walker as a sort of big brother.

Not that Jackson seemed to mind. Jackson wanted more from him. He'd finally stopped asking Kieran to abandon the Organization to join Jackson's security force, but now there were the poker games. Dinner was a must at least once a week. And of late Jackson had joined Kieran when he went to feed.

"Well, good evening," Jackson greeted.

"Hey," Kieran said. "What are you doing out of your office?" Jackson didn't spend much time on the casino floor any longer. He had staff who took care of that.

"I was just getting back from seeing Alex."

"How's he doing?" Dakota questioned. The soft concern in her voice was sincere. Everyone was still worried about Jackson's number one guy. Alex had been captured by the same group who'd held Kieran and Jackson years ago. He'd undergone some serious torture before they'd been able to rescue him.

"I'm not sure. I keep trying to get him to talk to me, but he still won't share what happened. I don't know what to do anymore," Jackson admitted. "I know there's something I can do. I just haven't thought of it yet."

Fuck, Kieran hated to hear that.

Dakota patted his back before nodding toward the bar. "Why don't you take Jackson to get a drink? I need to grab a shower and check in on those kids."

Kieran pulled her into his arms, grateful that he had such an understanding partner. Instead of acting jealous or demanding that he go upstairs with her, Dakota was urging him to spend time with Jackson, knowing what was needed. "I'll be up soon."

"Take your time," Dakota said. She turned to Jackson before giving his arm a pat. It hadn't been an easy relationship between the two of them. Jackson didn't trust shifters and Dakota was wary of such a powerful being. Slowly, they'd formed some sort of truce, though.

"You can go up with your girl," Jackson said. "I was just going up to get some work done."

"No," Kieran corrected. He threw his arm over Jackson's shoulders, steering him toward the small, intimate club located in the corner of the casino floor. "You're going to have a drink with your oldest friend while we try to figure out what we can do to help Alex."

The tension in Jackson seemed to leave him as he slumped against Kieran. "Thanks, K."

"You don't ever have to thank me. This is what friends are for." Look at him taking care of other people. First there'd been Dakota and now Jackson, not to mention the runaway shifter kids. He led Jackson to a familiar corner of the casino. Kieran loved the little jazz club. It was comfortable, with its soft music and nice staff. It was also where Dakota had appeared for the first time before he'd taken her up to his room. He liked to think of that night as their first date, although since she'd been stalking him, Dakota disagreed.

Tara, one of the waitresses, waved Kieran toward the back corner where he and Jackson would be alone. Tara knew both of them well. Neither of them would have to order as the bartender was already on it. Few tables were full, so they'd have plenty of privacy. Kieran ushered Jackson into one of the chairs before sitting across from him. He waited until Tara had dropped off both drinks before he pushed Jackson's to him and sipped his own. The whiskey was smooth going down and he was glad Dakota had suggested this.

He didn't get to spend enough time with Jackson or any other Walker. Kieran had questions that he wanted to ask but didn't know how to start. Instead, maybe he could help his friend and Alex.

"Alex isn't staying here?" Kieran asked. He'd thought that Alex stayed in the hotel as well.

"Not at the moment," Jackson said. "He has a suite, but I put him up in one of my houses. He needed to get away from the crowds."

"What can I do to help?"

"I don't know," Jackson said. "He needs more help than I can give him."

"I can find a professional for him," Kieran offered. "We have contacts through the Organization."

Jackson shook his head. "I'll find someone for him."

Kieran wasn't surprised. Jackson didn't trust the Organization and made no secret of it. "Anything else?"

"He's been asking about the wolf that was held next to him."

Kieran smiled. Alex had hated shifters before he'd been captured. It was good that he was thinking about one of the other prisoners. "He's doing well. I've been in contact with his Alpha and Damon assures me that he's recovering."

"Do you think he'd go see Alex?" Jackson questioned.

"Yes." Kieran was certain. "I can set that up."

"It might help," Jackson said. "We had each other. Maybe Alex needs to see someone who was there with him."

"I'll have him there tomorrow morning," Kieran promised.

"Thanks." Jackson downed his drink. "How're things going with you? Did you have your tests today?"

"Yeah. We still don't know anything more yet. We're still trying to see what was done to my DNA." Kieran signaled to Tara for another round.

"Well, if anyone can figure it out it'll be Dean. Mitch says he's good."

"Dean still wants to see you."

"No," Jackson stated. "I'll never be a test subject again."

"I understand," Kieran assured him. And he did. After what they'd been through, it was hard enough for him to allow Dean to take his blood. He only did it for Dakota's sake. If there was something wrong with him, he needed to protect Dakota.

"I'm sorry, man," Jackson told him. "I know you're looking for answers, but I just can't. I'd help you in any other way."

"Would you—?" He paused, waiting for Tara to set the new glasses down and take the others.

"What is it?" Jackson pressed after Tara had left.

"Would you answer some questions?"

Jackson stiffened. "About what?"

"What we are," Kieran whispered.

Jackson surprised him by laughing. "Of course. I forget that you haven't had anyone to talk to. Have you thought about contacting your parents? Your father?"

It was Kieran's turn to tense. He didn't like to talk about his family, although Jackson knew more about that part of his life than anyone else. Kieran had only been eighteen when he'd been captured by the shifters. He'd been cast out of his family when his father had decided that he'd supported a son long enough.

For some reason, Kieran's father was okay with his sisters staying home, but as soon as Kieran turned eighteen, a legal adult, he'd been kicked out. At least his father had given him money to start his new life. Of course, because Kieran had been captured, he'd never seen the cash ever again.

"It might help you move past things if you spoke to your dad," Jackson suggested.

"No. He sent me out into the world without any knowledge of how to take care of myself."

"He doesn't even know what happened to you."

"And he must not care, since he never tried to find me," Kieran pointed out. His family had money and resources.

"You're not an easy man to find."

"You did," Kieran reminded him.

Jackson laughed. "Fair enough. Ask your questions."

"I was just wondering about our abilities. Do you think I'm different from others like us?"

Jackson seemed to think about his question for several minutes before he nodded.

"That's what I was afraid of," Kieran confessed.

"I don't know why that bothers you," Jackson said.

"Because I'm even more of a freak?"

Jackson shook his head. "Aren't we all?"

"I can't even be a normal freak, though."

"You're a powerful fucker," Jackson said. "You might be the most powerful being I've ever seen. I'm not sure how that's a bad thing."

"I don't want it."

"Yeah, I know. Not that it matters. Things have happened to you beyond your control. At least you don't have to worry about that anymore. What really concerns you?" Jackson inquired.

"If I don't know what makes me different, how can I protect those I care for?"

"Like Dakota?" Jackson guessed.

Kieran didn't bother to answer.

"Your mate isn't helpless. She's strong and smart."

"She's not my mate," Kieran argued.

"Only because you're too worried about what might happen rather than taking advantage of what you have. That woman loves you. She'll do anything for you."

"That's what scares me," Kieran admitted.

"Kieran," Jackson said gently. "Stop waiting for trouble to happen. Embrace the life you have."

"I know." Kieran drained the remainder of his glass.

"You haven't fed, have you?"

"Not yet," he confided.

"You plan to go hunting?"

Kieran grinned. Jackson had stopped hunting to feed several years ago. Jackson kept donors on payroll for the purpose of being able to take blood without drawing attention to himself. Last month, though, he'd gone with Kieran, leading Jackson to recall why hunting down prey was so much fun. "I was thinking about it."

"Let's go." Jackson stood as he removed cash from his pocket. He didn't actually have to pay for the drinks since he owned the club, but he and Kieran always took care of the staff.

Kieran followed his friend as they strolled out the door toward the exit they'd both come in earlier. Jackson didn't hesitate to lead them through the dark parking lot to where the alley met with some houses. It was the trail that Kieran always took.

"Hold up," Kieran called. He had a method for how he liked to work. Closing his eyes, he used his senses to pick up the sounds and smells around him. He actually knew the area around the hotel pretty well and, thanks to his hunting and warnings to the criminals, he'd cleaned out at least a couple of blocks.

There was nothing several blocks to the north, but maybe something farther south. He motioned for

Jackson to listen. After a few moments, Jackson shook his head. Damn it, while Jackson didn't hear anything, Kieran was actually zeroing in on some sort of scuffle.

"Eight blocks south. Sounds like two men against one," Kieran informed him.

"Eight blocks?"

"Yeah."

"Damn," Jackson mumbled. "Let's go, then."

Kieran didn't waste time. He used his super speed to race toward what sounded like a mugging. He hated when people took advantage of others. There was enough evil in the world. Why did humans insist on preying on one another?

He rounded the corner to witness exactly what he'd thought.

Two thugs had a smaller young man up against a brick wall. A backpack had been ripped open, its contents scattered on the ground. The small teen was cowering from the bigger men. Both of the thugs were hearing hoodies — one dark blue and one black.

"Well, well, well, what's going on here?" Kieran drawled. Jackson hadn't caught up with him yet, but Kieran could hear his friend approaching.

"Stay out of this, man," Blue Hoodie demanded.

"I don't think so," Kieran countered. "There seems to be a party going on and I love to party." These idiots were human. They'd be tasty. He preferred to find his prey from the criminals in the city. When he fed from a human, they experienced severe flu-like symptoms. They'd be sick from twenty-four to forty-eight hours. It was the least they deserved for being assholes. At least Kieran didn't kill…anymore.

"Take off and mind your own business," Black Hoodie ordered. He turned to square off against Kieran, probably hoping to intimate him.

Too bad this moron had no idea who he was messing with. Kieran held up his hands. "Hey, just let the kid go. You don't need to do anything."

"How about we take what's in your wallet instead of this kid's?" Black Hoodie threatened.

"If you can get my wallet from my pocket, you can have everything in there," Kieran challenged.

The punk advanced, but Kieran remained, standing his ground. The thug in the blue hoodie had stepped away from the innocent teen and Kieran hoped the kid was smart enough to take off. To his relief, as soon as both attackers' attention was on him, the teen dropped, scooping up his belongings before hurtling in the opposite direction. That took care of the innocent one. Now Kieran could have some fun. He waited until the punk was just steps from him before he let his fangs drop and snarled. As expected, the guy froze.

"Oh, no," Kieran taunted. "You wanted to play. Let's play."

He moved quickly, closing the space between them and grabbing hold of Black Hoodie. He then tossed the guy behind him, just as Jackson turned the corner. In a beautiful move, Jackson caught the punk as he growled, looking fierce. Kieran laughed then launched himself at the second thug who'd begun to back away. He caught the guy and raised him a good several inches off the ground. He let the guy get a good look at his sharp teeth.

"This is my neighborhood," Kieran warned. "You don't do anything in my neighborhood."

The thug was already nodding. "You got it. Just don't kill me."

"If I ever see you back around here again, what I do to you tonight will seem like child's play."

"Please! Don't hurt me!"

A scream came behind them and the thug that Kieran held started to piss his pants.

"Fuck," Kieran said in disgust. He tossed the thug into the same wall he'd held the teen against. The guy landed hard before dropping to the ground. With the thug still dazed, Kieran crouched in front of him and bared the guy's neck for his bite. He struck quickly and the guy was beyond trying to fight.

He took six long deep pulls of sweet substance before releasing his prey. He took a little more than he normally would have, but Kieran hadn't fed in a while. Plus he was still sort of pissed at these two fuck-ups for threatening such a young man.

The thug was rolling onto his stomach, clutching it, just as the vomiting started. The warmth of the blood was already starting to work on Kieran's body. He was always so cold, except after a fresh feeding.

"Remember what I said," Kieran ordered. "If you come back to this area, I'll know. I have your blood now. I'll hunt you down and drink you dry." Okay, so he was over-playing it, but these idiots would never know that.

"We won't," the thug gasped then groaned.

Chuckling, Kieran headed toward Jackson where his friend was watching the first punk crying and sobbing. Jackson was leaning against a street light post, grinning.

"You look better," Jackson commented as Kieran joined him.

Already his strength was at full force.

"Nice catch," Kieran praised.

Jackson laughed. "Thanks for the food delivery. Great service."

Kieran could only shake his head. He liked hunting with someone else. It added more fun to an unpleasant task. Some people still thought of Day Walkers as vampires, but Kieran found that ridiculous. He didn't take blood because he was dead or undead. Walkers had a blood disease that ate up the good blood, requiring them to replenish what they needed. The sun didn't affect them and all the myths such as garlic, crosses and holy water were complete bullshit.

He knew, though, that the two thugs would believe the myths about vampires for the rest of their lives. Kieran had no problem letting the criminals spread rumors about vampires. Who was going to believe them, anyway?

"Ready to head back?" Jackson asked.

"Yeah. I want to see if Dakota checked on the kids already."

"Kids? Dakota said something about kids? Is there something you need to tell me?" Jackson looked smug.

"Vert funny," Kieran groused. "You know damn well we don't have any rug rats hanging around."

"Then tell me about the kids," Jackson said.

"Dakota came across three shifters in an abandoned building. One of them was hurt pretty bad, but all of them needed help. They'd been on the streets for a while. I'm worried they'll take off as soon as they get the chance. Dakota wants to help them and they've been through enough."

"What kind of shifters?" Jackson asked.

"Wolf, coyote and bobcat."

"Together?"

"Yeah, apparently they ran from a group home and from the Coalition. Right now, we have them under medical but I don't know how long that'll last."

"Well, let's go see what we can do." Jackson slapped his on the back as they started walking.

Kieran had no issue leaving the thugs behind suffering.

* * * *

Dakota hung up from speaking with Dean then walked over to stare out of the large window overlooking the Strip. It was a fantastic view of her city, a place that she'd spent her life protecting. There shouldn't be kids out there like Adam, Jeremy and Carmen, on their own, scared and afraid.

She wanted to help the innocents of her city and, if she couldn't do anything for the three teens, she wasn't sure why she gave so much to the Organization. There had to be a better place than a group home run by humans. Carmen had shared a little of what happened to shifters in the supposedly safe place. Dakota would let the kids run before making them return there. Although Jeremy would be the hard one to place anywhere. She'd been racking her brain but still hadn't come up with a solution.

The front door opened and she turned. Kieran strolled through and she knew right away that he'd fed. He was always paler than anyone else, but he had a pink tint to his cheeks and a healthy glow. He removed his jacket before tossing it across the back of the couch.

"Did you and Jackson have fun?" she asked, smiling.

"We did," Kieran replied. He walked straight to her to push her against the cool glass.

Since she wore just a robe after showering, it only took a tug of the belt to bare her body to him when he pulled. She licked her lips, examining him. He was in a mood from the recent feeding and she was going to benefit from him feeling so good. Dakota shuddered as he ran his gaze down her body.

"You smell good," he mumbled.

"Yeah?" she teased. Dakota leaned further into the window. They'd had special glass installed so they could keep the windows open and see out but no one would be able to see inside their suite. Kieran had a habit of taking her in open view of the window. Dakota didn't mind, but she also didn't want a child to witness what Kieran did to her. She let the robe fall to puddle at her feet.

"You look even better," he praised.

"What do I look like?"

"Like mine," he said then kissed her.

Dakota wrapped her arms around his neck, allowing Kieran to lift and pin her. The roughness of his jeans scraped against her with a unique sensation. It was hot having him holding her in place while fully dressed when she was naked.

"You want me," Kieran murmured, brushing his lips against her neck.

"Yeah, I do." She was already wet and hungry. He'd fed and now it was time for her to get dessert.

"What do you want me to do to you?"

Could she say what she craved? It was sort of kinky, but Kieran had never turned her down. "I want you to take your cock out and fuck me just like this."

He pulled back, grinning. She was surprised to see his eyes glowing a bright blue, like they did when he was taking blood. "Just my cock?" he asked.

"Yes," she admitted. "Keep the rest of your clothes on."

"I love you like this," he confessed.

"Then why haven't you put that nice, big, hard cock in me yet?"

He threw his head back, laughing, before hiking her up higher.

"Need help?" she asked, tightening her legs.

"Hold on to me so I can get my pants down," Kieran ordered.

She followed his command as he moved his hand under her until she felt his cock against her ass. Dakota wiggled, trying to get him where she wanted him.

"Stay still," he demanded. His smile on his face really did detract from the sharp words, making her giggle.

"Make me," she responded.

Kieran pressed her harder to the window and she stopped moving.

"Hurry," she pleaded. It was hard to hold back when the scent of his arousal was so strong. Plus, she really wanted to feel him inside her again.

Kieran pushed the tip of his cock inside before moving his left arm under her knee to spread her open. He kept his right hand at her hip. She tilted her back as he slowly entered her.

The cotton of his T-shirt and the hard denim of his pants rubbed as he thrust in and out. It was just as amazing as she'd thought it would be. Her pebbled nipples brushed against the top while he pounded her hard and her entire body rocked with the force of his movements.

Sweat on her back made it slick and she slipped up and down the window.

"I love being buried in your pussy," he said.

"Yes," she hissed. His cock felt huge. Maybe it was because he'd just fed or she was still sensitive from their earlier sex. Either way, she wasn't going to last long, and hopefully she could make it good for him, too. She squeezed her inner muscles on his shaft each time he plunged back in. Kieran groaned long and low. Yeah, that was what she wanted to hear.

"You keep doing that and I'll come," he warned.

"Fill me," she begged.

Kieran groaned again but sped up his thrusts. After that, Dakota could only hold on until she climaxed. Kieran plunged deep, riding her through her orgasm. She was exhausted and sated, but he felt so good and she didn't want him to stop.

"Get ready," he said. "I'm marking you from the inside out."

The shifter part of her rose. Dakota growled just as Kieran's rhythm faltered while he yelled. He pumped his seed inside and, yes, that was a claim she wanted. She might not be able to carry his scent, since he didn't have one, but his cum was at least going to stay with her for a while. Another kink they both shared.

Once spent, Kieran rested his forehead against hers. She closed her eyes, rejoicing in the mating they'd just shared. It hadn't been a full mating, as she craved, but she knew Kieran was hers.

"I love you," he whispered.

He didn't look at her when he said the words, but Dakota knew he meant them.

"Me, too," she said. "So much."

"I'm going to move us to the couch now. Hang on." He was still half hard and, if he wasn't ready to pull out, Dakota wouldn't make him. It was damn awesome being with a Walker. Even a shifter would be softening by now.

He sat with care, so as not to hurt her. Dakota rested her cheek on his shoulder while Kieran rubbed her back gently. They didn't need to talk. Not at times like this. Being alone with Kieran in the comfort of his arms was enough. Hell, she was pleased that he hadn't pulled out and gone to shower like other lovers from her past. It was still shocking that her big, bad Walker was such a cuddler.

No one else got to see Kieran like this. Or his other quirks, such as how he had piles of blankets on the bed. Only the softest and fluffiest were good enough. Kieran's body temperature being cooler than humans or shifters affected him greatly. Even in the middle of summer, he preferred long sleeves. At home, in their private suite, he mostly wore sweats. For Dakota, his clothing choices gave her easy access.

She sighed. Even though she wanted to stay like this for the rest of the night, there was still more work to do. There was always more work to do. Eventually, Dakota was going to steal Kieran away for more than a couple of days off. Shit, who was she kidding? The Organization controlled every part of her life. If they didn't want to let her go, they wouldn't have to. Very few agents within the Organization retired. No, the people that Dakota worked for had a hold on her and they got to tell her where to go and when.

"What are you thinking about?" Kieran asked.

"I want to go on vacation with you. Away from the city, just the two of us, without having to save people," she confessed.

"That would be nice. We could go to the beach, or up to the mountains, I'd love to show you the canyons where Angel lives."

Angel, Kieran's ex-partner, and fellow Day Walker. Dakota had only met her once but she'd liked the young woman. Angel had fallen in love and mated with a wolf shifter whose Pack lived in Texas. Angel had stayed with the wolves, which had given the Organization the chance to send Kieran and Remy to Vegas. To Dakota. "I'd like to see Angel again."

"Even if she's living with a bunch of dogs?"

Dakota laughed. "Don't let Remy hear you call the wolves that. And I'm not the one who has problems with shifters since I am one, after all."

"I thought dogs and cats didn't get along?" he teased.

She smacked his chest.

"I'll talk to Caspar," Kieran promised. "We'll get the time off."

"Really?" The excitement grew. Caspar thought of Kieran as a son and if Kieran asked, they'd be allowed for sure. She'd never had a real vacation before.

"If this is something you want? Yes, I'll make it happen."

Dakota squeezed him tight then began to rock her hips. Since his cock was still inside her, she could easily start a second round. Kieran grasped her hips as he leaned back on the couch.

The ringing of his cell phone jolted her.

"Fuck!" She dropped her head to his chest. "Don't answer it."

"You know I have to. Plus Jackson was going to see how he could help the kids we found today. It might be him."

"Damn it." She swung her leg and climbed off him. His cock was still wet from her juices and standing tall. "Don't lose that erection. I'm not done with you."

Kieran shook his head before digging into his jeans to get out his phone. She should have let him undress. Then the stupid cell wouldn't be within reach.

"Hello."

Luckily, she could hear both sides of the conversation.

"Kieran, it's Alpha Damon."

The scowl on Kieran's face was priceless. "What do you want?"

Dakota rubbed his arm. Even if Damon had worked with them in the past, that didn't mean that Kieran would ever do more than tolerate the Alpha wolf shifter.

"Jackson is not answering his phone," Damon said. "I've tried to contact him multiple times."

"He's been busy. I'm sure he doesn't have time for whatever werewolf bullshit you're calling about."

Damon growled low. "I understand your issues with shifters, but you're stepping out of line."

Kieran snorted. "Then don't call me."

"I won't make the mistake again. Just tell Jackson we had problems with two Walkers crossing our territory."

"What?" Kieran sat as Dakota stood. She made her way to the laptop that sat on the corner of the desk.

"Oh, now you're interested in what I have to say."

Dakota glanced up. It was apparent that Kieran was struggling with his words. "I apologize, Alpha. It's been a rough couple of weeks."

"I understand." Damon's voice held a hint of concern. "You've been through a lot. That doesn't mean we can't come up with a truce. We already stay out of the city as much as we can, but it would make things easier if we could share information."

She thought that sounded like a great idea. The Pack of wolf shifters lived out in the Red Rock area where they had open space and hunting room, but they were in a great location to see what was entering the city. She just didn't know if Kieran could ever get past his hatred for the Pack.

"We can discuss working together," Kieran conceded. "What can you tell me about the Walkers?"

"A couple of my young ones were out practicing their hunting abilities when they came across two men who didn't have a scent. They'd never met a Walker before so they were curious. They approached the men."

"Fuck," Kieran spat. He rose then began to pace.

"The Walkers attacked and a couple of the kids were hurt, but they managed to run away," Damon informed him.

"Okay. Have you told Remy?" Kieran asked.

"He's out there now," Damon answered. "Jackson's always been really good about monitoring the paranormals coming in."

"I'll tell him and we'll keep an eye out," Kieran said.

"I want them," Damon stated. "They attacked my Pack."

Kieran peered over at her and she shook her head. It wasn't within the rules of the Organization to allow that. Kieran pressed his lips together. Damn it, he loved to break protocol and she couldn't allow it this time.

"No," she pronounced.

"I'll see what I can do," Kieran assured Damon.

Dakota was going to beat him. They didn't need the shifters taking matters into their own hands.

"All right," Damon said. "Let Jackson know I called. I have my Beta and a few guards trying to track them down, as well. It'd be a lot easier if you Walkers had a scent to follow."

Kieran chuckled. "I know what you mean. But since I have you on the phone, I need you to do something for me."

"We're exchanging favors?" Damon asked.

Damn it, his earlier snark was going to bite him in the ass. "I have to deal with Dakota to even get you a chance with the Walkers. You owe me."

"What is it you want?" Damon inquired.

Unsure what to say, Kieran hesitated. Better just to be honest. "Alex is…struggling."

"Say no more," Damon irrupted. "I won't even count anything for Alex as a favor to you. He took care of my wolves."

"Right," Kieran said. "Alex needs someone to talk to. Jackson and I thought maybe if he could discuss things with someone who was there…"

"Sure, I'll make sure that Max goes over right away," Damon assured him.

"Thanks. So…one of us will call you back." He hung up while turning to stare out the window. There. He'd made nice with the damn Alpha. Hopefully, Alex would feel better after talking to Max."

"You okay?" Dakota walked over to pick up her clothes. She dressed quickly while watching him from the corners of her eye.

"There's not many of my kind in the world," Kieran said.

"I know."

"If these Walkers were attached to the Organization in any way, they wouldn't have attacked the shifters."

Dakota strolled back over to the computer. "I pulled up the database on Walkers we have. There are less than fifty families not connected to us."

"We have that information?" He turned to stare at her.

She nodded. "I didn't know about it before. Caspar gave me clearance a few weeks ago. I wish I'd had more time to look through it. I've been in the field every night."

"Guess we'll look at it now," Kieran said. "Would you mind making some coffee? And you should eat, too. It looks like it's going to be a long night."

"You don't want any food?" she asked. Kieran didn't live only on blood but also needed regular food and drink, too. Since he'd hunted earlier, he still needed dinner.

"Yeah, let's just order room service. That way, we can get to work," he suggested.

Dakota grinned. The hotel had wonderful restaurants and, since neither of them cooked well, they often took advantage of the perk of living there. When they'd discussed moving from the last room, Kieran had brought up living in a house. Dakota was glad they'd held off. She didn't want to admit that she'd gotten spoiled. Food and drink at the tip of her fingers, daily housekeeping and several shops just downstairs. She felt like a kid in a candy store. "I'll start the coffee and place an order."

He seemed distracted as he nodded.

"You didn't answer my question if you're okay or not," she pointed out.

Kieran lifted his gaze to hers. "I have a bad feeling."

Well, that was not what she wanted to hear. "We'll figure it out."

Chapter Four

Kieran waited until Dakota had walked into the kitchen before collapsing in the chair in front of the laptop she'd set up. He hadn't even known that a database of all Walkers existed. His family would be on there. The family that had sent him away. Dakota, Caspar and the others knew nothing about his family. Smith wasn't even his real last name. This fucking night was turning into a complete mess.

His hand shook as he scrolled down the page until he saw what he was looking for.

Argent

"Fuck," he murmured. Just seeing the last name made him sick. It wasn't as if he didn't often wonder about his parents or siblings. It hadn't been his choice to leave, though. Fearing the power Kieran might gain with age, his father had sent Kieran away to start his own life. Kieran still didn't understand why he hadn't been accepted as his sisters had been. He hadn't been shown much love by the patriarch of the family growing up, but Kieran thought his mom would have argued for him. Instead she'd merely turned her back and watched as Kieran's dad had sent him away.

Kieran hadn't been ready. Having been home schooled and having lived his entire life inside the mansion, Kieran hadn't been prepared for the real world. That was how the shifters had captured him in the first place.

"K?"

Dakota's hand came down on his shoulders and he jumped.

"What is going on?" she demanded.

Kieran knew he wouldn't be able to hide his feelings from her. He was going to have to admit a few things that he'd held back. "My family is on this list."

She shook her head. "I looked at the names when you were on the phone with Damon. Smith is missing from the list. I figured Caspar didn't put them on there to protect you."

"My last name isn't Smith."

He stared at the screen instead of looking at her. He knew Dakota would be angry. He hadn't lied to her, but Kieran also had hidden everything.

"I... I was going to tell you one day," he whispered. "They... I mean my real last name —"

"No," Dakota cut him off. "Don't tell me."

Kieran snapped his head up. "What?"

"That's not who you are anymore." Dakota set the mugs down that she'd been holding before lowering herself between his legs. "I know who you are, Kieran Smith. You're my lover, you're Remy's best friend and a great agent. Caspar is more your dad than the man who raised you. I don't care what any of those files say. I know you."

Relief flooded him. He grabbed Dakota, yanking her into his lap.

She wrapped her arms around his neck. "I know you."

Kieran kissed her hard. He'd feared the day that he'd have to confess who he really was. The Argent clan was rich, powerful and respected. They also didn't believe as the Organization did that paranormals and humans could live in peace. The Argents thought that they were better than humans.

"Now how should we start?" she asked, once they'd separated.

"It'd be easier if we knew what they looked like," Kieran said.

"Call Jackson," she said. "I'll get a hold of Damon and see what the kids said. We'll go through the files and pull out all the photos that match the description. Tomorrow, we'll pass out the pictures to the teams and have the entire city searched."

"That's a good idea," he admitted. It made him feel better to have a plan.

"So separate the list. You can take your own family and that way I won't know which of the twenty-five it is. Then we'll get to work."

"Thank you," he murmured.

"Baby, you don't have to thank me. I'll always be on your side."

He nodded.

"Okay, I'm calling Damon back." She rose before placing a soft kiss on his lips.

Kieran picked back up his cell as she moved around. She pulled her bag onto the couch, setting up her own laptop on the coffee table. Kieran stood, taking her coffee to her. Dakota smiled at him even as he heard the phone ringing.

With her busy, getting to work, he sent an email to Jackson with all the information he had so far and what the plan was. Jackson had said that he was going to be in his office, so he should still be awake. Then he looked back at the list of names.

"I'll take the first twenty-five and you take the last," he called to Dakota.

She gave him a thumbs-up before her call was answered.

Kieran tuned out their conversation and decided to just get it over with. He clicked on the link under *Argent*.

The first thing that he saw was the family crest.

Kieran ran his fingers over the screen. The familiar circle with ancient symbols and fangs caused an ache deep in his heart. The last time he'd seen that had been the night the shifters had taken him prisoner. He'd never seen his necklace again.

"Thanks, Damon," Dakota was saying.

He blinked away the tears that had started to gather. He wouldn't miss a family who had sent him into the hands of monsters. In the ten years that he'd been held captive, plus the more than a dozen since his rescue, the Argents had never searched for him. With their connections, it wouldn't have been impossible for anyone in the family to locate them. Kieran was certain they'd never tried.

Dakota hung up so he had to tear his gaze from the laptop. "What did he say?"

"Two men, both in their late twenties or early thirties."

"If they're Walkers, it would be difficult to tell how old they really are," he reminded her. Now that he'd reached adulthood, his own aging process had slowed down. Luckily for him, since he was with a shifter, the same applied to Dakota.

She rolled her eyes. "They look to be in their late twenties or early thirties."

"Sorry," he said. "Go ahead."

"One of the teenagers said he thought they might be related since they had such similar features."

"That's helpful," Kieran commented. "We can narrow it down through that alone."

"Yeah, that's what I was thinking," Dakota agreed. "Both have dark brown hair, hazel eyes, clean cut and dressed in dark suits that appeared expensive."

"That at least gives us a place to start." Kieran was glad they had something. He really didn't like the thought of unknown Walkers in his city. He knew Jackson would feel the same way.

"I told Damon I'd email him some possibilities."

Kieran nodded. He glared back down at his screen. Instead of going further into his family, he needed to concentrate on the task at hand. Now that he knew about the database, he could look into what the Argents had been up to without him later, if he wanted. Maybe he'd just forget it all together. Only pain could come from what he'd find, although he was curious about his mom and sisters.

"Food's about here," he mumbled. The scent of their dinner coming had his mouth watering. Plus he'd heard the *ding* of the elevator.

"It's weird when you do that," Dakota stated, standing.

Kieran ignored her. He backed out of his family's file and opened the next.

Chapman

Dakota moved around the living room, setting his plate and a bottle of beer at his elbow before returning to the couch. The Chapmans weren't as notable as his own family, but they had a long line of descendants, so it took time to go through each photo.

The Organization had done their homework. Not only was there a profile of every person, but their closest friends as well. The subject's likes, interests, hobbies, criminal record, suspected activities and more was included. Kieran found it creepy that someone was actually actively stalking the Walkers.

Some of the updates were just weeks old.

Finishing the Chapmans, Kieran moved to the next family. He hadn't found anyone so far that matched. He hoped to have more luck.

Dakota had ordered steak sandwiches and French fries, so he began to pick at his food as the aroma called to him. Happy with her choice, he looked over at her.

Her long hair was still mussed from their earlier activities and her clothes were wrinkled. It didn't look as though she cared much about her appearance as she ate with one hand while typing with the other.

She'd surprised him bringing up her desire to go away with him. Dakota was so dedicated to her work it was nice to see that she was willing to step away once in a while. When they'd met, she'd even lived in the Organization dorms, not even having her own place.

Kieran had moved out as soon as he'd been able to.

He'd hated having all the other agents around him so much. Dakota loved it. They were such opposites, but somehow things were perfect between them.

"Quit staring at me," she said, without even looking up.

Kieran grinned. "I can't help it. I'm enjoying the view."

She glanced up. "We need to get through at least half the lists so we can send the information to Jackson and Damon before we get some sleep."

"Fine." He returned to work. She was right. The sooner they finished, the quicker he'd be holding her in bed.

Halfway through his portion of the list, Jackson replied to Kieran's email. He clicked on the icon, bringing it up.

Good, Jackson was going to have his men start patrolling the city. Given that Jackson ran the most successful security company in the country, it would help having his assistance.

"I'm switching to wine," Dakota announced. She stretched after standing up.

Kieran glanced over at the window. Dawn was approaching and, since they'd both be on shift that night, they'd have to go to bed soon. "Sounds good."

He'd only found a dozen possible suspects, which surprised him. He'd supposed there'd be a lot more, but he'd noticed a pattern. Walkers gave birth to three times as many females as males. "How many do you have so far?" he asked.

"Maybe twenty," she replied. She frowned, glancing up at him. "There's a lot more females who would meet the age range."

"I noticed that, too," he admitted. He wasn't really surprised that Dakota had caught the same unusual thread. She was a brilliant agent.

"Is that normal?"

Kieran shrugged. "I don't know. I only have sisters, but I do have several male cousins."

"You have sisters?" She stopped pouring the wine to look at him.

He shifted in his chair. "Uh, yeah."

"Huh." Dakota shook her head then finished pouring the drink. He waited for her to say more, but she remained lost in thought. Since he knew she wouldn't be shy of asking him something she wanted to know, Kieran let her think.

When she still didn't say anything once she'd set his glass down next to him, he patted her ass.

Dakota glared at him. "Another hour then we'll turn in."

"What if I don't want to wait that long?" he teased.

She waved at hand at him then flopped back down on the couch. "Get back to work."

Damn, he did love when she turned bossy. His cock even perked up a bit. He'd stuffed his cock back in his jeans even though he'd left them unbutton. He would be so easy to just slide them down his legs and be on the couch with her.

"An hour," he repeated. "You're not any fun." His complaint drew a smile from her.

* * * *

Dakota rolled over and turned off the alarm before it woke Kieran. They'd worked until eight that morning and had sex in the shower before climbing into bed together. They'd managed to find almost seventy possible subjects who she'd emailed to Jackson and Damon.

She wanted more than six hours of sleep, but she'd already scheduled a meeting with Dean about the shifter teens before work.

"Why are you getting up?" Kieran muttered.

"I have to meet with Dean. I want to check on the shifters before I give Caspar an update. I'm hoping he'll agree not to call in the Coalition."

He grunted. Kieran had no love for the Shifter Coalition. Dakota wondered if she would have been offered a job with them if she hadn't been obligated to the Organization. It might have been fun to work within the agency.

"What time are you going in?" she asked, leaning over to run her hands over his bare chest. Even though his skin was cooler than hers, she couldn't resist touching him.

"Remy's meeting me here after he gets up." Kieran still had his arm over his eyes so Dakota couldn't see those beautiful blue peepers. "We'll check in with Jackson and Damon before we go in."

"Are you going to tell Caspar?"

He groaned but sat up against the headboard. She should have probably let him sleep, but she loved how cranky he was when he first woke. "Yeah, I figured he probably already knows we were using the database this morning. If I don't, he'll think I'm hiding something and probably have me followed again."

"That might be fun," she commented. "Last time, it was great training for a new agent."

Kieran scowled. "I almost threw him off the roof of a building."

Dakota laughed. Caspar really did do everything in his power to protect Kieran, even if Kieran didn't want protection. "Yes, well, try not to do that again."

"Just go!" Kieran grouched. "Remy won't be here for another couple of hours."

"You could get up and finish the search," she suggested.

Kieran swiped at her, but Dakota rolled off the bed, dodging him. Strolling to the bathroom, she knew she had his full attention. He never could resist her naked and wet. She barely had time to turn on the water before Kieran embraced her from behind.

"I thought you were going back to sleep," she teased.

"Someone got me up," he replied, dragging his morning erection over her ass. "And now that someone needs to take care of me."

Dakota reached between them to palm his cock.

"Yes," he hissed, before nipping along her shoulder.

"Get under the water," she ordered. Dakota moved away and pushed him into the stall. Steam rose, but since Kieran loved the water as hot as they could stand it, Dakota knew he wouldn't have any issues with the temperature.

As the water cascaded down his broad shoulders and pale chest, Dakota lowered to her knees. Kieran kept his gaze on her the entire time as Dakota wrapped her hand around the base of his erection. She ran her palm down his length then back up before leaning forward to take the tip of his cock into her mouth.

"Please," he murmured.

Dakota slid down his shaft closing her eyes to enjoy the hard silkiness. He tasted so good. Kieran might not have a scent but his flavor burst onto her tongue. She knew how to bring him off, too. Sucking and licking him, she used her other hand to pump. Kieran slapped his hands onto the tile to keep upright. Yeah, he'd begun trembling. Dakota was in power here.

It was easy to ignore kneeling on the tile as she worked him over with her mouth. Kieran's grunts and moans spurred her on until he came.

"Come up here," he demanded, helping her rise.

His lips covered hers as he plunged two fingers deep inside her pussy.

Dakota grabbed his shoulders as she rode the climax that exploded from her. She laughed, throwing her head back. "That was fast."

Kieran frowned. "I can go again."

"We don't have time." She pushed him away so she could actually shower and not just play.

"I'll wash your back," Kieran offered.

"I'm not falling for that again." Dakota picked up a washcloth and the soap and scrubbed down as Kieran picked up a bottle of shampoo.

They quickly finished up and Dakota turned off the water as Kieran passed her a towel. Dakota glanced at the clock. They'd actually been in there longer than she thought.

"Do you want me to order you up some breakfast?" Kieran was toweling off his pert ass and Dakota wished she could take him back to bed.

"I'll grab something on the way."

"Okay." Kieran tossed the towel into the hamper before strolling out naked. "I'll at least get you coffee."

Dakota smiled after him. Kieran had a mother hen instinct that no one else knew about. He concerned himself about her eating enough all the time. Once she'd wiped most the water off, she strolled into the bedroom and to the closet.

She'd go with jeans today instead of slacks. If she got the chance to head out into Pack territory to check out where the Walkers had been seen, she was going to. Maybe the two strangers were just in town to do some gambling and partying, but then they should have avoided the local Pack.

"Did you check your email?" she called out.

"Not yet." Kieran stepped up behind her.

"Jesus!" She jumped and almost fell. "Don't do that!"

"Here." He passed her a full cup of coffee. "I'll go check it now."

"Thanks," she said before kissing his cheek. Dakota took her mug with her as she walked back to the bathroom. She took sips in between braiding her hair and applying her makeup.

"Jackson might have someone who saw the two men," Kieran suggested, strolling in to lean against the door jamb. "They're sending me the security cameras to look at."

"That's good." Dakota finished up her morning brew. "Keep me informed. I might go out to see Damon."

"Don't go alone," Kieran said. "At least take the bear with you."

Dakota pushed her empty cup into his stomach before shoving past him. "My partners have names, you know."

"I'm aware of that."

"So you should use them." Dakota didn't think Kieran actually hated the two agents she was assigned to, but he could make more of an effort to get on with them.

"I let them work with you. I think that's good enough."

Dakota stopped, still bent over where she'd been about to pick up her boots. Sometimes the shit Kieran said shocked her. Was he serious? "You *let* them work with me?"

He nodded before setting her cup on the dresser. "If they disappeared, they wouldn't be able to work with you."

"Kieran," she snapped. "You can't say that."

The look that came across his face was pure cockiness. Dakota knew she shouldn't let this conversation go, but she didn't have the energy to fight with him. Kieran had his moods and sometimes it was better to ignore them as long as possible.

"I have to meet Dean." She finished getting ready and stood.

Kieran blew out a long breath. "I shouldn't have said that. I'm sorry."

Oh, he was so cute when he pouted. He never quite pulled off the innocent look, but still he tried. She stalked over to him. Pushing on his chest, she backed him into the wall. "I like my partners. I want you to get to know them better. I'm going to invite them over, as well as Remy, for dinner this week."

Kieran whined. "Come on! I said I was sorry."

"No." She shook her head. "We're going to get along."

"Fine."

"Now, give me a kiss," she demanded.

That Kieran did, happily. A little too happy since they were both breathing hard by the time she ripped herself from him.

"You're an asshole," she accused.

"Yep."

"I'm leaving." If she didn't, she'd start to laugh and, really, she couldn't encourage his behavior.

"I'll probably see you later."

"Because you'll show up where I'm at?" she asked. Dakota still hadn't figured out how Kieran always knew where she was.

"I have to talk to Caspar," Kieran reminded her.

"All right." Dakota walked from the bedroom with Kieran on her heels. "I should be able to break away in a couple of hours."

"I put your travel coffee cup by the door."

"Thanks." Dakota whirled around, grabbed his waist, yanking him into her. She nipped his bottom lip. "Behave."

Kieran was chuckling. "Never."

She grabbed her weapon, keys, phone and coffee from the table. Kieran really was good about taking care of her. Instead of her spending ten minutes searching the suite for all her stuff, he always put it right where she could find it. Dakota had gotten lucky with him.

Without another word, she dashed out of the door. Dakota scrolled through her phone as she stalked to the elevator. There weren't any missed calls, but Dean had texted her twice. She responded that she was on her way before pocketing her cell.

The ride downstairs was quiet, giving her time to prepare for her day. There was a lot that she needed to fit in, as well as being on patrol. She might need to talk to Caspar about switching up rotation so she'd be able to look for the Walkers.

By the time she was in her vehicle, driving toward the office, she'd worked out everything she needed to do. It was a good thing that both she and Kieran kept vehicles at the hotel, since she'd left the SUV from the previous night in the garage to go with Kieran.

It didn't take long before she was pulling onto Falcon Ave where the Murphy Institute was located. Dakota slowed down when she spotted the same dark sedan behind her that she'd glimpsed leaving the hotel. There wasn't anything out of the ordinary about it — just some gut feeling that she needed to pay attention.

Only her training had had her even picking up the tail.

Dakota pulled into the fast food restaurant on the corner to see if they followed. The sedan continued down the street and she blew out a sigh of relief. The last thing she needed to worry about was someone following her. Kieran would hit the fucking roof. The sedan had kept enough distance that she hadn't been able to read the license plate. Since she was already there, she pulled up to the drive thru and ordered several breakfast sandwiches.

After she'd paid and pulled back onto the street, Dakota glanced around the neighborhood. Her office was only about six blocks down, so if she had been followed, they would be close by.

She didn't spot the vehicle and was relieved. Maybe she was being overly cautious. The last couple of weeks since they'd captured the shifters responsible for Kieran's years of torture had been hard on them all.

Dakota stopped in front of the guard gate and waved before she was allowed in. Parking in one of the open spaces, she noticed that Dare and Gabe were already there. They weren't on shift yet, so that surprised her. She grabbed the bag of food and her coffee before walking over to the stairs. Her relationship with Kieran had affected how she entered and exited the building.

Kieran's fear of being trapped in an elevator had rubbed off on her. Besides, as good as the food was at the hotel, she could use all the exercise she could get.

"Hey," she greeted two agents as they went down while she walked up.

"Afternoon, agent," they responded.

One was human and the other some sort of bird shifter. Kieran was the only Walker they had on staff there. Actually, Kieran was the first Walker she'd ever met. Jackson and his group had been living and operating right under her nose and she'd never known.

"Agent Reese." Caspar stood at the fire exit door, holding it open.

Oh, shit! "Uh, hello, sir." She dipped her head. He was her boss now and Dakota was sleeping with the man who Caspar loved like a son. "Something wrong?"

"Where are you headed?"

"I'm meeting Dean," she answered. "But I was going by the medical wing to drop off some food first."

Caspar nodded. "The shifter kids."

"Yes."

"Dean's there. I'll walk with you."

Alarm flooded her. "Did something happen to them? Are they all right?"

"They're fine," Caspar said.

He adjusted his long strides so that Dakota wasn't having to jog to keep up with him. She knew something was going on if she was getting a personal escort. She wanted to press for more answers, but Caspar was still an unknown to her.

As they made their way through the halls, she watched him out of the corner of her eye. It wasn't until there were no other agents around that Caspar stopped. Dakota wasn't surprised.

"You opened up the database for Walkers," Caspar said.

"I did."

"So did Kieran," Caspar added.

"He's supposed to come talk to you later today," Dakota said. She didn't want to step on Kieran's toes.

"Why don't you tell me now?"

Well, damn, Kieran's not going to like this. She eyed Caspar, noting for the first time that he didn't seem to be in a very good mood. *Double damn.* Dakota moved to lean against the wall as she explained about Damon's call. She outlines their plan even though Caspar's expression grew tighter.

"That's everything so far?" Caspar asked once she'd finished her verbal report.

"Jackson is sending some footage for Kieran to review. It might be of the Walkers," she said.

"Fine." Caspar nodded.

Dakota didn't know if she was dismissed so she stayed right where she was.

"Did he tell you anything about any Walkers in the database?" he asked softly.

"You mean his family?"

"Yes."

"I had suspected that you would have removed his family to protect him. Especially when I didn't see Smith under the index."

"And?" Caspar pressed.

"He told me that wasn't his real last name."

"He said that?" Caspar sounded shocked.

"Yes."

"I'm surprised," Caspar admitted.

"Oh, I was, too. He started to explain, but I could see that he wasn't ready. I told him that it didn't matter. I know who he is now, so it doesn't matter where he came from."

Caspar straightened while he stared at her.

"What?" She wanted to snap at him, but this was her new boss.

"Do you mean that?"

"Of course, I do." No hesitation. Dakota wondered about the family who had thrown Kieran out for no reason, but that didn't matter to her. Kieran was hers now and that was what was important.

"I always thought you'd be good for him," Caspar murmured. "Did he seem okay?"

"I don't know if he opened the file or not. We split the list and I suggested he take the half with his family."

"That was smart," Caspar praised. "I'll do some following up. You can tell him you spoke with me but I still expect a full report from him."

"Okay." At least he wasn't ordering her not to talk to Kieran.

"You supposed to be patrolling tonight?"

"Yes, sir," Dakota replied.

"I'll rearrange the schedule. See to the teenagers you found then work on this new development. I'll keep both your and Kieran's teams on it. I don't want the Pack or Jackson getting to them first."

Dakota nodded. "Yes, boss."

"Things would be a lot easier if Jackson would just work with us," Caspar muttered.

She laughed. "If he wasn't so close to Kieran, I don't think we'd know anything he was doing."

"I can see that. Okay, agent, you're free to go."

"Thank you." She rolled the tension from her shoulders as she stalked away. That had been one uncomfortable conversation. Every time she had to speak with Casper, she felt as though she was being judged.

There was only one more corner to turn before she reached the medical wing. Instead of them taking the stairs, Caspar had been leading her the long way around. She heard the shouting and picked up her pace.

Dean was standing in front of Adam, holding up his hands. Jeremy was cowering against the door. She didn't spot Carmen and that worried her. Dakota didn't think they'd move too far from her.

"What's going on?" she asked, reaching them.

Adam turned. His face was red and he was breathing hard. "You liar," he screamed.

Dakota stopped walking in shock.

"You promised!" Adam shouted. "We trusted you."

"Wait a minute! You need to calm down. I haven't lied about anything," Dakota said. "Just tell me what's going on."

"We won't go with them," Adam said. "I don't care what you try to do to us. We aren't going."

Dakota glanced up at Dean in question.

"The Coalition is here for a different matter and they overheard some talk about the kids," Dean explained. "One of the agents came down to see if he could help, but when the boys saw him, they freaked out."

Shit! Dakota didn't need this. "Where's the agent now?"

"He went back down to the cells to finish his paperwork. He really was just trying to be friendly. He felt really bad about upsetting the kids," Dean said.

"We're not kids," Adam yelled.

She'd had enough. "Yes, you are. And we're trying to help you. How is your acting like this good for Carmen? Where is she? And look at Jeremy."

Adam glanced behind him and guilt flashed over his features. "J! I'm sorry." Adam grabbed the coyote shifter then tugged him close. Jeremy nodded but was still shaking.

"Let's go inside and discuss this calmly," Dakota ordered.

Dakota was pleased that Adam kept his arm around Jeremy, speaking quietly to him. She didn't want to be too hard on any of them, but they couldn't act up, either. The Coalition technically had the right to step in and deal with the entire case. Dakota didn't blame the agent for trying to help. That was his job, after all.

"I brought breakfast," Dakota said, following them into the room.

Carmen was huddled at the top of the bed with the blankets wrapped all around her.

"It's okay," Dakota assured her. "Just a misunderstanding. Let's eat and talk this out."

Adam led Jeremy over to the bed, where both teens climbed up. Dakota waited until the shifters were settled before setting the food on the end of the mattress and digging through.

"Smells good," Carmen whispered.

"I hope you're hungry," Dakota said, smiling.

"Yes, ma'am," Carmen replied. Jeremy had his head buried in Adam's neck as he breathed deeply.

"Here." Dakota passed the food to Carmen and let her give it to the two boys.

Once everyone had a couple of the packages, she tossed a few to Dean before sitting in the chair with her own food.

"Can you explain to me what happened?" Dakota asked.

"It's my fault," Adam said. "We saw the coyote shifter and heard he was from the Coalition and I freaked out."

A coyote shifter — that was interesting. Dakota really wanted to talk to this guy.

"Do you know the Coalition agent? Is it the same one who you dealt with before?"

All three teens shook their heads.

"That doesn't surprise me. He's from Arizona."

Dakota nodded. "Okay, everyone eat and we'll work this out."

"Thank you," Adam whispered.

"Of course," Dakota said. "We really are here to help."

Jeremy lifted his head for the first time. "Was he really like me?"

"A coyote shifter?" Dean asked.

"Yeah." Jeremy nodded.

Dean glanced at Adam. "I don't know. I'm human so I can't tell."

"He is," Adam said. "I could smell him. It's like the scent of a wolf but different." Adam looked to Jeremy. "Just like you."

"I've never met another coyote shifter before," Jeremy murmured.

"Once we figure things out, maybe you'd like to talk to him? Ask him a few questions?" Dakota offered. She didn't care what the Coalition agent said. She would make it happen if that was what Jeremy wanted.

Jeremy looked at Adam.

"I think it would be a good idea," Adam said to his friend. "Who knows when you'll get this chance again? I can stay with you when you do if you want."

"Thanks," Jeremy said. Finally he started to open his breakfast.

"You know the guy's name?" she asked Dean.

"Luca Perez," Dean answered.

She hoped that this Luca guy turned out to be all right. She wasn't above using Kieran to threaten the guy if need be.

Chapter Five

Kieran had finished going through the database on Walkers and had switched to the footage of a gas station. Jackson's contact thought he might have had a visit from the two Walkers they were looking for. Kieran was hoping to match a face from the camera feed to those he'd viewed in the database.

Remy knocked on the door before opening it and strolling inside. Kieran glanced up and glared at him. Then paused the video.

"Where'd you get the key?" Kieran asked.

"I have my sources," Remy said.

"You stole it," Kieran guessed. "Damn it, Remy."

"I wanted to check out the security at this so-called great establishment," Remy defended. "They could use some work."

Kieran was certain that Jackson was going to hear about this. Jackson and Remy still had a rocky relationship, which made things difficult for Kieran at times.

"Whatcha doing?" Remy asked, walking over.

"Jackson's guy might have something. I'm checking some video from a station just outside town. Between here and the Pack," Kieran said.

"Did you send over the photos?"

Kieran pointed to the extra laptop. "It's in your email. Check them out."

"Got coffee?"

"Of course." Kieran waved him off toward the kitchen. With their schedule, it wasn't unusual for them to drink coffee most of the day and into the night. He actually preferred working nights since he could hide in the shadows easily, but he knew it was harder for the shifters.

Remy came out of the kitchen area, holding a mug of coffee and eating an apple.

"That was Dakota's," Kieran complained.

"I'll buy her another one."

There wasn't much of a response to that. While everyone thought Remy was the responsible partner, Kieran knew the truth. Remy was just as big of a troublemaker as he was. Angel had actually been the one who had kept them in line.

Kieran restarted the video on his laptop. There had been a couple of guys who had entered the gas station, but no one that had stood out to him so far. This really was his best lead and he needed to hit gold.

"You didn't pick up anything from the scene?" Kieran asked without looking at his partner.

"Just the scent of the teens' fear. I was hoping that there might be some of the Walkers' blood or something, but I couldn't pick it up. I don't see why these guys even went after the kids. It's obvious they didn't pose a threat."

"Some people are just assholes," Kieran commented.

"Yeah but their actions announced their presence to the Pack," Remy said. "That wasn't smart."

"Unless they think shifters are beneath them," Kieran pointed out. It was a common thought of Walkers, like his family. Kieran had never even met a shifter before he'd left home. He knew his father did business with some, but Kieran had always been kept away from his dad's associates.

Remy growled.

"I'm not saying it's right," Kieran assured his partner. "It's just how some Walkers think."

"Yeah, well, you might be an asshole, but even you aren't that much of a bastard," Remy stated.

Kieran grinned. "I'm glad you think so."

A knock came at the door and Kieran frowned. He didn't scent anyone out in the hall. Remy glanced over at him and he shook his head. They moved together to cover the room. Remy stood back with his weapon in his hand as Kieran walked to the door. He didn't need a gun or any weapon. There wasn't much that could take him out.

He glanced through the peephole and snorted. He waved Remy off before opening up to Jackson. Jackson grinned in the hallway.

"Jumpy much?" Jackson taunted.

"I didn't hear the elevator," Kieran admitted.

"I know," Jackson replied. He looked past Kieran to Remy. "And I didn't lift an employee's key card."

Remy laughed. "My entrance was much better."

"Don't fuck with my employees," Jackson said.

"Then they should be more careful," Remy replied.

Jackson glanced at Kieran.

Kieran shrugged.

"I wouldn't put up with him if he wasn't your partner," Jackson griped.

"And his best friend," Remy added.

Jackson growled as he stepped inside the room. Kieran closed the door behind him. Eventually the two of them were going to have to work things out. Kieran needed them to, anyway. Jackson and Remy would be thrown together more often than not.

"Card," Jackson demanded, holding his hand out.

Remy slapped the small plastic square into Jackson's palm. "Sure, I wasn't going to keep it."

"Just so you know," Jackson informed him. "My security caught the swipe. I allowed you to make it to the elevators."

"Sure," Remy said.

Jackson's nostrils flared. Now was not the time for this shit. There was plenty of work to do. If Jackson was going to be there, he could help them.

"Come on, guys," Kieran said. "We don't have time for this."

"Have you found anything on the footage I sent you?" Jackson asked.

"Not yet," Kieran admitted.

"What can I do to help?" Jackson offered.

"Can you two work together?" Kieran questioned.

Both men nodded. "Go through the pictures with Remy and let him know if you recognize anyone. If there's someone that you know, we need all information that you have."

"No one I know would do this," Jackson stated.

"Because they wouldn't beat up a bunch of shifter teenagers?" Remy asked.

"No," Jackson said. "Because if they know me they wouldn't enter my city without my permission. It has to be a walker who I've never dealt with before."

Remy snorted. "You're not the king of Las Vegas."

"As far as the Walker society goes, I am. It's common knowledge for my people to know that I police this entire city. Plus, both the Coalition and Organization have offices here. That's one of the reasons most paranormals won't stay around for long. Too many people looking over their shoulders."

"So you think whoever attacked the kids is up to trouble?" Remy grew serious. Kieran approved. Even if Remy enjoyed fucking with Jackson, Remy still did his job, and did it well.

"It concerns me," Jackson stated. "They made a stupid move. They're either cocky or dangerous. I think it might be both."

"Let's see if we can narrow down any of our possibilities," Remy suggested.

Kieran let them get to work. He had to rewind the video since he hadn't stopped it when Jackson arrived. As he waited, Kieran rubbed his tired eyes. He hated this part of an investigation. If Kieran had his way, he'd stay on the street and let other people take care of the research.

"I've met the first three," Jackson was saying. "It wouldn't be them. They know I'd kill them."

Kieran had to smile, listening to Jackson. Kieran would have never believed when they'd both been starved, beaten, tortured and abused that they'd one day be sitting around a plush suite working alongside one another. It was just too much to think about, so he stopped rewinding the damn footage to rewatch it.

Remy and Jackson were making progress on at least eliminating suspects. Kieran didn't feel as if he was making any progress at all. That changed, though, when he recognized two men enter the store.

Kieran sucked in a breath.

"What?" Remy asked, glancing over.

"Did you find something?" Jackson jumped up.

"I…" Kieran paused the video. It couldn't be. No way, oh, God please let his eyes be deceiving him.

"Kieran." Jackson placed his hand on Kieran's shoulder.

"Dude, you turned even paler than normal." Remy leaned over his screen. "Do you know these guys?"

Kieran couldn't tear his gaze away from the monitor. It had been so long. Still, the two men looked exactly the same. Fuck, they even dressed the same.

"Kieran?" Remy shook him gently. "What the hell is going on? Jackson, do you know them?"

"No," Jackson said. "I've never seen them before."

Kieran reached out and touched the frozen image. This was one of his worst nightmares. His past colliding with his current life.

The laptop lid snapped shut and Kieran jerked back. He glanced up and both Remy and Jackson were staring at him with twin looks of concern.

"Take a deep breath," Jackson commanded.

Kieran wasn't sure if the followed directions, but after a few moments, the dizziness seemed to fade. Jackson's hand felt hot and tight. Kieran jumped to his feet, pushing away from both the table and his friends.

"Just calm down," Jackson said. He was holding up his hands toward Kieran. "Whatever, or whoever this is, it'll be okay."

Would it? Kieran wanted to ask. He couldn't get his mouth to work, though.

"Should I call Dakota?" Remy asked.

"No!" Kieran roared.

Jackson and Remy both jumped back.

"I mean no," he said more calmly. "I'm…"

"Tell us," Jackson said. "Just get the words out. It'll feel better once you say the words."

Kieran shook his head.

"Kieran," Jackson said sternly. "Who are those men?"

"My cousins. They're my cousins."

* * * *

Dakota tracked down the Coalition coyote shifter Luca Perez in the cafeteria. He was a good-looking man, probably in his thirties. He had dark hair and eyes. If Dakota wasn't absolutely and one hundred percent in love with Kieran, she might have been tempted to flirt with the agent. As it was, she carried over a bottle of water and motioned to the chair across from him.

"Mind if I sit?" she asked.

He lifted his head and smiled. "Of course not. Please."

"You're Luca Perez?" she confirmed. "From the Lake Worth Coalition office."

"I am," he replied. "And you are?"

"Dakota Reese. I'm the one who found the teenagers yesterday. The ones that you tried to talk to earlier."

He used a napkin to wipe his mouth before nodding. "I apologize for scaring them. I was only offering my help."

"It's okay," she said. "Are you still willing to help?"

"Of course." Luca glanced around. There weren't many people sitting close by as most of the agents were out on patrol. "What do you need?"

"One of the kids is a coyote shifter," Dakota explained. "He's never met anyone of his species before."

"Really? What about his parents?" Luca asked.

"He ran away from a group home with the others. I don't know his story yet, but he'd like to talk to you. Ask you a few questions."

"Yes!" Luca exclaimed. "I'll do whatever I can to help. Why'd they run?"

"I have some people looking in to it," Dakota replied. She'd already sent Gabe and Dare to dig around and see what they could find out. If something bad was happening at the group home, she'd see the place shut down.

"Good." Luca nodded. "What about the other two?"

"The coyote shifter is Jeremy. Adam is a wolf shifter and Carmen a bobcat. Adam is kind of their leader and he'll probably be with Jeremy when he talks to you."

"That's fine." Luca waved his hand. "I actually work with both a wolf and many feline species."

"Great." Dakota was happy that she wouldn't have to convince this agent to talk to the teens. They were going to need all the help they could get. Maybe Luca would even have some recommendations for placing Jeremy.

"Is there some place comfortable where I could talk to them?" Luca asked.

Dakota had to think about the question. She could put them in her office, but that might seem too formal. The rooms in the medical wing would just serve as a reminder of what the teens had been through. There was a lounge that the agents used when they were between double shifts or just needed a break. She could clear that out and let the shifters talk there. "Yeah, I think I can find you the perfect place. Give me about fifteen minutes then come to the second floor."

"Sounds good," Luca agreed. "Can I ask you a question before you leave?"

"Sure," she agreed.

"You're the shifter that's dating the Day Walker, right?"

She stared at him across the table. It was common knowledge that she was dating Kieran and of course the rumors about the two of them were spreading quickly around the Organization. It still felt weird that people talked about her personal life, though.

"I didn't mean to be rude. I was only curious. I've never met a Walker before."

"Few people have," she replied.

"A couple of years ago, a Walker saved a family from being slaughtered when their car broke down on the side of the road. I've tried to find the Walker to thank him. It's like he just disappeared."

"And you think it was Kieran?" she asked. "Why?"

"I spoke to his partner, Remy," Luca admitted. "They were in town hunting the shifter that almost killed that family. From what I've managed to put together, Kieran saved them and killed the shifter."

It was quite possible. "He wouldn't admit it if you asked. He doesn't talk about his cases."

Luca grinned. "That doesn't surprise me. I'd still like to meet him, if he wouldn't mind."

"I'll tell you what," Dakota said. "You help me with the kids and I'll make sure Kieran talks to you."

"Cool!" Luca nodded. "Although I'd help, anyway."

"I know. But this way, Kieran will be more willing to talk to a shifter."

"Oh." Luca's smile fell. "Is there a problem? I don't want to be in the way."

Oh, yeah, he wouldn't know about Kieran's past. "He has a history with shifters."

"I'm sorry. I didn't know. Just forget about it," Luca said.

"No," Dakota responded. "This will be good for him too. Let's go talk to the kids then we'll figure out how to get Kieran and you together."

Luca appeared uncomfortable.

"Really, it's okay."

"If you're sure?"

Dakota was. She tried not to push Kieran when it came to accepting the shifters, but he also had a hatred toward the Coalition. Luca seemed like a pretty good guy and he might be a good contact for Kieran between the Coalition. "Give me fifteen," she said then took off to get things in order.

Pleased with herself, Dakota hurried to the second floor to kick any agents out of the lounge.

Luckily, there was only two guys and they didn't mind giving her the room. Dakota wrote a quick note and hung it on the door before shooting Dean a text to bring down Adam and Jeremy. Then she called her lover.

"Everything okay?" Kieran said in greeting.

"Yeah, fine," she responded. He, on the other hand, didn't sound okay. "What's going on?"

"Nothing," Kieran said quickly. Too quickly.

"Don't lie to me."

"Just... I'm trying to figure it out. Can you give me a couple of hours? I'll tell you everything then."

"Oh, okay." Dakota wished she was there with him. It was obvious that he was going through something. "Did you look in your family's file or something?"

"No." Kieran lowered his voice. "I just recognized someone. Can I call you back?"

"I guess." Dakota hated not knowing what was going on with him.

"Dakota," Kieran said before she could hang up.

"Yes?"

"I need you to be careful, very careful. There's something happening."

"So tell me what's going on," she pleaded.

"I will," Kieran said. "Just give me some time. Watch your back."

A chill ran down her spine and she remembered the feeling of being followed earlier. Maybe she should mention it.

"Promise me," Kieran said.

Yeah, she wasn't telling Kieran about the dark sedan. He didn't sound like he could handle any more at the moment. "Promise. I have a few things to do around here before Dare and Gabe get back."

"Be careful."

"You, too," she said. She disconnected the call as she heard approaching steps.

"Hey, Dakota," Dean said. "I got your text. The boys are ready."

Jeremy was wringing his hands together. He looked so lost Dakota's heart went out to him.

"It's going to be okay," Dakota said. "I met Luca. He's a really nice guy."

"Maybe this is a bad idea," Jeremy whispered.

Dakota met Adam's gaze and motioned for him to go into the lounge. "I'll bring them back up when we're done," she promised Dean.

"Okay, see you soon." Dean nodded before walking back down the hall.

Once alone with Jeremy, she smiled at him. "Just relax and talk to Luca. He was pleased that you even asked."

"Really?"

"Yeah. I know coyote shifters aren't that common. He's probably just as excited to talk to you as you are him."

"Actually, I am even more so," Luca said, coming up behind them.

Jeremy jumped.

"Hey, sorry," Luca said to Jeremy. "I thought you heard me walking. I brought some candy bars and cokes."

"Th...th...thanks," Jeremy stammered.

"No problem." Luca nodded toward the lounge. "Ready?"

"Sure." Jeremy moved inside.

"Appreciate this," Dakota whispered.

"Are you coming inside?" Luca asked.

"I think they might talk more freely without me. I'm just going to be down the hall if you need anything," she said.

"All right," Luca agreed.

He shut the door behind him and Dakota listened as he introduced himself to Adam and Jeremy. Adam was doing the talking for now, but she hoped that with time Jeremy would take advantage of this opportunity.

Not wanting to eavesdrop, Dakota strolled down toward the spare offices. Her laptop was in her backpack and she needed to check in with her partners.

Plus, she hadn't heard from anyone about the Walkers. There was plenty of work to do as she waited.

* * * *

"You didn't tell her," Remy said quietly. He was sprawled out on the living room floor with an empty plate on one side of him and photos on the other.

Kieran didn't look at him or Jackson, who was working on the couch. Much like Dakota had the previous night, Kieran hadn't moved from his place at the desk. It had been hours since he'd recognized the two men in the video feed and he still felt numb.

"You're going to have to tell her," Jackson commented.

"I know," Kieran managed to respond. He was still trying to come to terms with what he'd seen. His cousins, Marcel and Elijah Argent, were in town. They'd been the two Walkers who had attacked the wolf shifter kids.

"It's not your fault," Remy said for what felt like the hundredth time. "Whatever they're up to can't have anything to do with you. You haven't seen them in over a decade."

"What if they're here for me?" Kieran asked. "Then anything they do is because of me."

"No, it's not." Jackson sounded firm.

"Why would they even be here for you in the first place?" Remy questioned. "How would they have found you?"

Kieran waved at the papers strewn around the room. For the first time in his life, he'd told someone about his family. Who he really was. What they'd done to him. Remy had been shocked. Jackson hadn't said anything and, by the look on his face, Kieran guessed that he'd already known. Kieran didn't know how he felt about that. "I always knew they'd find me if they really wanted to."

"It still doesn't make sense," Remy pointed out. "If they know where you are, why didn't they just drive into town and see you? Instead they creep in by walking through Pack territory. They haven't even tried to contact you."

"He has a point," Jackson said.

"Oh, so now you two can agree on something?" Kieran griped.

"We just want you to listen," Remy argued. "Just listen."

Kieran stood. The muscles in his neck were tight and his entire body ached. He'd been holding himself in the same position for way too long. Maybe they were right. If he could just think clearly, he could come up with a plan.

He paced to the window and peered out. Below him, hundreds of people were going about their day unconcerned about what might be stalking them. Kieran made certain when he hunted, it was only those who caused harm to others, and he never killed. A few sips and Kieran was good for a couple of days. Marcel and Elijah, at least when Kieran had been around them, hadn't appreciated human life. Their father was Kieran's dad's brother and both of the elder Argents had very specific beliefs on how feeders were treated.

It wasn't until Kieran had been out of the house that he'd realized the man and woman they all fed off probably hadn't been there by their choice. Since Kieran had been forbidden from speaking with the couple, he hadn't tried.

He regretted how much he'd taken for granted under his father's hand. From the moment he'd been old enough to crave it, Kieran's attention had gone into trying to gain his father's favor. Kieran used to dream of a time that his dad would say he loved him or was proud of him. But Kieran had never heard those words.

Kieran sighed. Why was he feeling like that thirteen-year-old boy who had both feared and despised his father? Kieran was too old, too powerful, to allow such foolishness. He lifted his gaze to the horizon. There was a storm coming. Not only could he see the dark clouds rolling in, but he felt the electricity in the air. If he was outside, he might be able to touch it. The storm called to him. Kieran wanted to go out and stand out in the open.

"I'm listening," he finally said to his two friends.

"You don't belong to them," Jackson said. His reflection in the window showed him approaching Kieran slowly. "You're not the same man they sent away."

"I want to believe that," Kieran confessed.

"Believe it," Jackson ordered. "Who you are now is a man who protects the innocent. You're an agent, friend and lover. You don't prey on those who don't deserve it. You are not a monster — you're a hero."

Kieran snorted.

"You got me through the hardest time of my life. I would have died in that hellhole we were held if not for you. You're my brother," Jackson continued. "My brother."

Kieran closed his eyes. The words shouldn't have affected him so much, but they did. His entire being warmed, just like when he took blood, and he turned to pull Jackson to him.

They hugged. It wasn't the brief manly embrace they'd exchanged in the past. Instead, Kieran allowed Jackson to hold him up. Not for long. Kieran would be steady again. He just needed this moment.

He didn't know how long he clung to Jackson. Finally, he managed to straighten and step back. "I won't let them hurt anyone else," Kieran vowed. "I'll kill them first."

"You won't be doing it alone," Remy said. He flanked Jackson before reaching out to grip Kieran's shoulder. "Just tell us what to do."

No, Kieran was longer the frightened boy he'd once been. Even though he'd fought against it, somehow, Kieran was part of a family. An unusual one, sure. A mixture of Walkers, shifters and humans. He might not have ever wanted the bonds to another, but they were there.

"If they're looking for me, I say we let them find me," Kieran announced. He glanced over at Jackson. "We need a poker game."

"Poker game?" Jackson repeated with obvious confusion.

Kieran didn't hide his grin. Jackson loved poker and had been trying to teach Kieran. There was a bi-monthly game between Walkers Jackson wished Kieran would join. Kieran's impatience seemed to always get the better of him. "Yes."

"Why?" Jackson pressed.

"Because both Marcel and Elijah have a weakness for gambling. They used to hold games in the back of a rundown human bar. I never attended any, but I remember some of the rumors."

"Rumors?" Remy asked.

"They didn't only play for money."

Remy jerked back. "What does that mean?"

"From what I can remember, every once in a while, they, along with my uncle and father, hosted a high-stakes game. *Very* high stakes."

"Which were?" Jackson questioned.

"Life and death," Kieran whispered. He couldn't look either of them in the eye as he spoke the next part. "They'd invite a shifter or human and play for that person's life. If the shifter or human lost, they forfeited their life and a real hunt took place."

Remy gasped. "*Hunt?*"

"Yeah," Kieran confirmed. "My family released the loser into a specific location then hunted him down. Like an animal."

"You never took part in this...hunt?" Remy sounded like he didn't want to even ask the question.

"No."

"Why not?" Remy crossed his arms over his chest.

Damn it, there was no good answer. He wouldn't lie to Remy, though. "I wasn't old enough. My family wouldn't have allowed it. The only reason that I even picked up on the rumors was because I used to eavesdrop on my father when he was in his office."

"They talked about it?" Remy asked.

"More like bragged," Kieran replied.

Remy growled before he turned and paced. "I hated your family before today, but now... Everything I've found out, I want to rip their throats out."

Jackson chuckled. "You're not alone there."

Kieran shook his head. "We need to know what they want first."

"Of course." Remy waved his hand. "But after?"

"After?" Kieran repeated. "After, we'll have a hunt of our own."

"And if they just want to bring you home? Or have a message from home?" Jackson inquired. "Can't hunt them down for that."

"True," Kieran conceded. "But they will still have to answer to Damon for attacking members of his Pack."

Remy nodded.

"But I know my family. If they just wanted to talk to me, they wouldn't have sent Marcel or Elijah. Those two enjoy getting their hands dirty. I would expect one of my sisters to approach me," Kieran admitted.

"What should we do first?" Remy asked.

"You need to call the Alpha and let him know what we've discovered. The Pack needs to stick close together. They need to be on the lookout, especially the ones that come into the city," Kieran said. He glanced at Jackson. "They have to be staying somewhere. We need their names and photos sent out to all your contacts. No one has the Strip covered like you."

"What are you going to do?" Remy questioned.

Kieran strolled back over to the files on his family. "It's time I found out what dear old dad has been up to while I've been gone."

"I'll start another pot of coffee," Remy announced.

Jackson waited until Remy has left the room before leaning over the desk. "And Dakota?"

"I'll not hide anything from her. Being a shifter would put her in enough danger. But me loving her? They'd go after her without question."

"I can help you protect her," Jackson offered.

Kieran barked out a laugh. "She'd gut us both."

Jackson merely lifted an eyebrow.

"Yeah," Kieran said. "Do it. Whoever it is had better be good. If she spots them, they're in for a world of hurt."

"I have just the guy. Someone who needs a reason to live again."

"Not Alex," Kieran said.

Jackson grinned.

"Bad idea," Kieran warned. "He's not recovered. You told me that yourself. Hell, he won't even come back here and he loves this place."

"He will if I need him. If you do."

"It's dangerous."

"Yes, it is." Jackson's agreement was gleeful.

Kiran let Jackson spin away and pull out his phone. He just knew that he was going to get his ass handed to him by Dakota. Somehow, she would figure it out. Still, what other choice did Kieran have? Even as well-trained and strong as Dakota was, she was no match for a Walker.

No, he was doing what was best for her. Whether she liked it or not.

Chapter Six

Dakota watched the sheets of rain that poured from the sky. The rumble of thunder loud above her with furious flashes of lightening gave her glimpse of the angry weather. Las Vegas hadn't seen a storm like this in a long time. She should get in her vehicle and start the drive home, but she couldn't stop staring.

Some part deep down felt as though the storm was a warning.

It was ridiculous. Mother Nature couldn't warn her about anything. but the feeling wouldn't leave. Instead, every instinct was screaming at her to prepare for an attack. Dakota was too smart an agent to ignore the sense of danger.

She clicked the key fob and unlocked an SUV before climbing behind the wheel. A deep breath told her that no one had been inside or around recently. That helped her relax her shoulders and ease the tension. She hadn't gotten a chance to go out into Pack territory, but a text from Kieran had her needing to head back to their suite.

Kieran needed to tell her something and she just knew that it was bad.

Her hands were steady as she put the key into the ignition. She turned on her vehicle before checking the mirrors then backed out carefully. There was no one else in the parking garage. It wasn't the end of shift so most agents were still out on patrol. Dakota drove out, pausing to wave at the guard, before turning left to take her back home.

She darted her gaze all around her.

Not only was she looking out for the blue sedan from that afternoon but also any signs of danger.

Nothing.

Dakota had no idea why she felt so uneasy.

Still, Kieran had told her once again to be careful and watch her back until she returned to him. Dakota would heed his advice.

The entire drive seemed to take double the time than usual. It wasn't just the rain slowing her down. Taking note of everything and everyone on the street was nerve-racking.

She blew out a long breath when she finally pulled into the private parking garage. Kieran was close by. She might not be able to feel his presence, but she knew he was only a few steps away. Dakota was home.

Even though the casino and hotel should be safe, she wasn't going to take any chances. Dakota peered around the small area. The parking garage was almost full, but no one was hanging around or walking toward the doors. It was probably due to the weather. Still, she couldn't shake the eerie feeling.

Dakota grabbed her bag and exited her SUV before locking it with the remote. She made a mad dash across the lot until she reached the glass door. It had rained so much that the sidewalks and entryway was flooded.

"Here you go!"

She glanced up and saw an attractive man holding open the door for her.

"Thanks." She stepped in with him at her heels.

"You're welcome," he said with a smile. "I thought it didn't rain here."

Dakota laughed. She had to shake off the water before brushing down her bag. "It's unusual enough. But just gives us more reasons to stay inside and spend our money."

The man laughed. It was a nice sound, deep and friendly. Wow, he was really good-looking. He even seemed somewhat familiar. "You must work here if you're already trying to get into my wallet."

"No." She waved her hand. "I just know this town."

He leaned against the wall, drawing her gaze to his long muscular body. His blue eyes were sharp and sparked with intelligence. The hairs on the back of her neck stood.

"Are you staying here? In the hotel?" she questioned.

"Actually down the Strip. I can't afford the accommodations here. But the casino is beautiful and I've had some luck at the tables," he answered.

"Oh, so you've been in town long?"

"A few days," he said vaguely.

Dakota knew there was a camera in this hallway, but for some reason she had the feeling that this man was deliberately keeping her there. Trying to appear normal, she took a few steps to the side so she could see more of the other guests. Where the hell was the security that she knew had been placed all over the floor?

"Vacationing or business?" she questioned.

"Oh, we're here for fun."

"We?" she repeated. "I'm sorry, I didn't catch your name."

"Because I didn't give it to you, Dakota."

Oh shit! Dakota backed away but felt another presence coming up quickly behind her. That was when she noticed that the man she was talking to didn't have a scent. "We've been looking for you. Where's your partner?"

"Right here, shifter."

Dakota turned. She'd already known that he was close. "I appreciate the two of you finding me," she said, keeping her voice calm.

They both laughed. "Oh, we've found you. But you're not who we really want," the first guy said.

This is about Kieran. It has to be.

Dakota lifted an eyebrow. "Oh? My feelings are hurt."

The second man grabbed her arm, hard. "We want you to give your boyfriend a message."

She tried to yank away, but he only dug his fingers deeper into her flesh. Damn it, that was really going to piss Kieran off. "And what message is that?"

"Tell Kieran to come and find us," the first one responded. "Or we'll find you again. Next time you won't be around a building full of people."

"Why wait?" she taunted. Dakota was not going to show these two monsters any fear. "I don't have plans now."

"We enjoy the hunt," the first man stated.

Dakota bared her teeth. "I do prefer to stalk my prey."

"You're nothing to us." She was shoved into the wall. Dakota grunted from the impact before sliding down.

Fuck, she'd forgotten how strong Walkers were. "Just tell Kieran what we said."

The rushing of feet could be heard right before a roar sounded. Well, it appeared her backup had arrived. Too bad Dakota was still too busy to get up and chase the Walkers.

The Walkers took off, running through the back door. Dakota attempted to push herself up, but strong hands came down on her shoulders. She lifted her head and growled.

"It's me," Remy said. "Don't bite."

"Oh." She plopped back down. "Where's Kieran?"

"He, Jackson and about half the security staff chased after Kieran's cousins. I don't think they'll catch them, though. He should be back any minute."

Dakota waved at the floor. Fuck, she was dizzy. Even if she wanted to Dakota didn't think that she'd be able to catch up. "I'll just wait here."

"Good idea." Remy was on his knees beside her. "You hit your head pretty hard."

"Yeah." She rubbed the side of her head. "Fucking Walkers."

"I'm not going to tell Kieran you said that. He was so pissed off running down the stairs that his eyes were glowing. I swear he didn't even touch the ground. He fucking flew."

"He's fast," she agreed.

"I'm a fucking wolf shifter and I couldn't even keep him in my eyeline. He's more than just fast."

Dakota patted Remy's knee. She was already healing and really didn't want to be on the floor when Kieran got back. "Help me up."

"Are you sure?"

"Dude, I don't know how often they clean the carpet here. Help me up."

"Good point." Remy stood before reaching down and lifting her to her feet.

"That's better." Dakota's vision wavered, but Remy kept his hand on her elbow.

"I think they're coming back. I can hear the humans huffing and puffing," Remy said.

"Good."

"Brace yourself," Remy whispered.

She didn't have a chance. One minute she was turning to the door and the next she was lifted up into Kieran's strong embrace.

"Are you okay?" Kieran demanded.

"Yeah, sure, fine." Dakota rested her head on his shoulder. He was solid and could watch her back for a few minutes. She closed her eyes as a roll of nausea hit. "Just stand still a minute, will ya?"

"I am," Kieran promised.

Dakota dug her nails into her own palms. The pain helped to clear her head. She didn't understand what was happening. Dakota had already felt her healing abilities kick in. But instead of growing steady and strong, she was having trouble keeping her eyes open. "K—"

"Yes, baby?" Kieran whispered. "Dakota?"

"Something wrong," she managed. Fuck, why was her tongue getting bigger?

"Dakota!" Kieran yelled.

She couldn't see his face even when she was laid down on her back.

"Jackson! Get over here! Dakota, please, look at me."

Dakota tried to lift her hand, but her body was too heavy. She knew something was wrong but couldn't figure out what had happened. The Walker had tossed her pretty hard, but she was a shifter. She'd been shot, stabbed and torn by claws. These wounds were nothing.

"Fuck! She's been poisoned," Jackson screamed. "We need to get her upstairs. Now!"

Poisoned? How in the hell had the Walker done that? Instead of fighting what was going on inside her body, Dakota thought about what had happened. She'd made a lot of mistakes, even though she'd been aware of her surroundings. She should have realized right away that the man who held open the door hadn't had a scent. Also, she'd found him attractive. Dakota was going to have to confess that to Kieran.

Shit, she was just ready for this day to end.

"How long will she be out?" Kieran asked for the tenth time.

"A couple of hours," Jackson replied just as calmly as he had before. "And you pacing next to her isn't helping anything."

Kieran gazed down at Dakota from where he'd laid her in the middle of the bed. She wouldn't be cold, but that hadn't stopped him from burying her under the mound of blankets in some sort of weird comforting gesture. The suite was cool for a shifter and she might not be sick, but she was injured.

Or fucking poisoned.

He couldn't believe it.

"How the fuck did this happen!" he bellowed.

"Kieran." Jackson gripped his shoulder. "You saw the security tapes same as me. They had this planned. It was smart, fast and brilliant."

"I'm going to rip their hearts from their chest while they're still alive. After I chomp off every single fucking finger. Then I'm going—"

"Dude!" Remy bitched, coming into the room. "Save your rage for your cousins and come out here. Mitch and Alex are here and Mitch thinks he might have found something."

Kieran couldn't be blamed for the rumbling growl that sat inside his chest. Jackson pushed him out in the main room with a tight grip as Remy shut the door behind them. He tried to turn around, but Jackson wouldn't let him.

"Keep the door open!" he demanded. If he wasn't in the same room as his lover then he at least wanted no barriers between them.

Remy sighed, but did as ordered.

Standing next to his couch was Jackson's second in command, Alex, and his brilliant IT specialist and hacker, Mitch. Alex's normally neatly styled black hair was mussed. He had a at least a week's worth of scruff, making the Walker looked unkempt. Mitch, the spirted black-and blue haired young Walker, wore green skinny jeans and a long-sleeve black shirt. He was bouncing on his toes.

"Hey, Kieran," Mitch greeted. "Is Dakota going to be okay?"

Kieran nodded. "It doesn't appear to be deadly poison. One just to make her sick."

"That's good. I was going over the security feed and I pinpointed the moment he injected her."

"Show me," Kieran demanded.

Mitch waved him to the laptop that had been set up on his coffee table. Kieran stepped forward, but Alex stepped in the way. Kieran lifted an eyebrow at Alex.

Now was not the time for anyone to fuck with Kieran. He was seconds away from losing control. He didn't even need an excuse to unleash the rage inside him.

"I'm sorry I wasn't here," Alex said. "That I hadn't arrived. I was already on my way when Jackson called me but if I had been here…"

"You're here now," Kieran said. Alex's concern eased some of Kieran's fury. "This isn't your fault. And you're here now to take care of her. All that I ask is you don't let her out of your sight. I'm trusting you with her."

Alex nodded, his shoulders drooping. "I won't fail anyone again."

Alex walked away before Kieran could speak again. It was obvious that the stress and strain Alex had been through was still strong and holding the Walker back. Maybe Jackson had been right. Alex needed something to bring him back from the brink of torment.

"Are you ready?" Mitch asked. He'd taken a seat on the couch so Kieran joined him. "Watch just before he pushes her into the wall."

A growl slipped out.

"I know." Mitch patted his hand. It would have been funny in any other circumstance. The small, young Walker comforting him. "Look at his left hand."

After Mitch hit Play, Kieran did as directed. Marcel held Dakota's arm in his right hand. Kieran had already seen the bruises on her skin. But once Mitch had told him what to look for, he saw the moment that Marcel brought his left hand up, syringe concealed, the needle shoved into her neck. Half a second before Marcel threw her.

"God damn it," Kieran murmured. "I'm going to enjoy killing him."

"I called Caspar," Remy said. He stood behind Kieran's shoulder. "This is an attack on an agent. I had to, so don't look at me like that."

Kieran continued to glower at his partner.

"He's on his way and bringing someone with him," Remy said.

"I don't want more fucking people in my suite!"

"Too bad." Remy was not concerned with Kieran's anger. Of course they'd been partners for so long that they both knew he'd never actually hurt Remy.

"How'd they get in?" Kieran asked Jackson.

Jackson shrugged. "Walked in the front door."

"What?" Kieran and Remy asked in unison.

"Cameras picked them up about half an hour after Dakota left. They didn't act out of the ordinary until right before Dakota arrived. That was when Marcel caused the distraction as Elijah waited for your woman. It was planned and smart. They knew who she was."

Yeah, they did.

"There's nothing in the file that shows they've been in town or even close," Remy stated.

"They don't have the same power here they do at home. There, they control everything, other Walkers, humans, cops and even the few shifters. Here, they'd have to play by someone else's rules," Kieran said.

Mitch spoke up. "I'm still trying to track them. I hacked into the traffic cameras and am running a new program."

"If anyone can, it'll be you," Jackson praised his young Walker.

"I guess we don't need to set up the poker game," Kieran said.

"We'll see," Jackson corrected. "You're going to learn to play, no matter what."

Kieran rolled his eyes.

"It's good for you," Jackson said. "You need more hobbies."

"Hobbies?" Kieran snorted.

Jackson pushed aside the laptop and sat on the coffee table right in front of him. "There will be times in your life when you get tired of living. Our existence is a long one. I think that's one of the reason your father and uncle turned to hunting for fun."

"There's no excuse," Kieran muttered. God, he hated thinking about his childhood and family. It worried him that he came from vile creatures.

"It's not," Jackson said. "But I've seen it many times by many of us. Humanity is something that we've never had. Over the years, it's common for our kind to stop caring about much of anything. You have Dakota, your friends and your job. That might not always be enough. But for as long as you have things that you enjoy, you won't turn into one of those monsters."

Kieran finally understood why Jackson had been so intent on getting him involved with the casino. "Fine." He could give his oldest friend this one thing.

"Good." Jackson grinned. "Now as Mitch tries to track your cousins down, we need to figure out what Dakota was injected with."

Dakota. His heart ached. It hadn't been when she was out on patrol or trying to save an innocent life that had injured her. His cousins had gone after her because she was his.

"Can you run more than one program?" he asked Mitch.

"Of course." Mitch leaned forward. "What do you need?"

"All the footage for the past two days around here. My cousins had to have seen me and Dakota together. If we can't track their movements from leaving here, maybe we can figure out where they've been."

"That's a good idea," Jackson praised. "Now you're using your head."

Someone knocked on the door and Kieran stiffened.

"It's Caspar," Remy called, running to the door.

Kieran needed to get hold of himself. He should have known before his boss stepped out of the elevator.

"Hey, boss," Remy greeted, after he'd opened the door.

"Remington." Caspar's deep voice carried through the suite. "Is Dakota well?"

"She's asleep right now."

"Kieran?" Caspar questioned.

"I'm right here if you wish you speak to me and not about me," Kieran shouted.

Caspar snorted before pushing his way past Remy. "There is no reason to yell, young man. I can hear just fine even with my human ears."

Kieran grinned, ignoring the shifter who followed Caspar inside his suite, to taunt his mentor. "Are you sure? I hear that's the first of the senses to go."

The familiar narrowing of Caspar's eyes eased him some. If Caspar could still act like a father to him, then things were going to be all right. *Dakota* had to be all right.

"Come here, Kieran," Caspar ordered.

He started to shake. Kieran wanted to go to him, but he couldn't take a step. No, his legs wouldn't work. "I…"

Caspar didn't wait any longer. He stomped across the room, grabbed Kieran's arm, before dragging him into the bedroom. Alex stood next to the bed and Caspar pointed at him to leave.

Kieran didn't even look after the Walker. Instead, as the door closed, Caspar yanked him into a hard embrace.

"It's okay, my boy," Caspar murmured. "Everything is going to be just fine."

He broke. Kieran didn't even remember the last time he'd cried. Sometime in the hell of those cells that had once held him. Ten years of torture had taught him that tears never did him any good.

"Come." Caspar nudged him to sit on the bed. "Sit by Dakota."

Kieran lifted his head, but Caspar was the one who dashed at the watery bloody streaks on his cheeks.

"Sit." Caspar pointed.

Kieran put his head to the headboard before taking Dakota's hand in his. He was burning with embarrassment from breaking down in front of his boss.

"Listen to me," Caspar ordered. "And don't speak until I'm done."

Kieran nodded.

"It's time you embrace who you are," Caspar said.

He opened his mouth to ask what Caspar was talking about, but his mentor held up a hand.

"It's obvious now that whatever Bradley and the doctor did to your DNA has changed you. I've been waiting for you to come talk to me about the changes you're experiencing, but you seem intent on ignoring all the signs."

Yeah, Kieran couldn't argue with that.

"You're afraid that you're turning into a monster," Caspar accused.

He was.

"So, instead of embracing the power that you know hold and using it to your advantage, you're running from yourself."

Is that what Kieran had been doing? He thought back on the past six weeks. It seemed that Caspar had been paying better attention than Kieran realized.

Caspar stood in front of him with his hands on his hips, glaring at Kieran.

Kieran peeked up. Even though Caspar was human, he was still a force and Kieran might tease his boss, but he also respected Caspar's abilities. Kieran had never feared Caspar. Not even when he'd been rescued and unable to feed or protect himself. His mentor and rescuer was the first person who Kieran had ever trusted. He was the dad that Kieran had been craving.

It was no secret to anyone in the Organization that Caspar loved him. And even though Kieran had never said the words, he felt the same about Caspar.

"So, what do I do?" he finally asked.

Caspar's smile was wide.

"First things first." Caspar glanced at Dakota. "How was the poison administrated?"

"Injection."

Caspar nodded. "I thought so." He circled the bed to kneel on the other side of Dakota. He lifted her eyelid before laying his hand over her heart.

"What?" Kieran asked.

Caspar cut him a fierce look and Kieran sat back. He didn't want to get in the way. "Your family has a history of using a blood agent on shifters."

Kieran frowned. "Blood agent?"

"A mixture of Walker blood and other things. It's been found in the shifters that they've attacked. If the shifter isn't killed within an hour of receiving the injection, they wake up. They'll have similar effects as they would if a Walker had fed from them several times in a row."

"*Fuck.*" Kieran didn't even take Dakota's blood, even though it was possible. Shifters usually got a headache and some weakness, while humans had full flu symptoms.

"She'll be okay." Caspar repeated what everyone was telling him. "You need to concentrate on hunting down your cousins and making sure they don't hurt anyone else."

"We're taking care of it." Kieran had confidence in the people he'd chosen to help.

"I brought you someone to assist you."

"Yeah, like I hadn't noticed you bringing another fucking shifter into my suite."

"Dakota didn't have a chance to speak with you about Luca, I assume?" Caspar questioned.

"No."

"She met with him today. He's helping with the shifter teens. Dakota was going to make you meet him, anyway."

"Why?"

"Ask him."

"I hate you," Kieran grumbled.

"No, you don't."

Kieran glared then leaned down to brush the hair off Dakota's forehead. "Wake up soon." He wouldn't put it past Dakota to come up with a reason for him to have to meet a shifter if she believed it would do him some good. She was always telling Kieran that his past didn't have to define his future.

Caspar led the way out of the bedroom. Alex remained standing next to the door and Kieran nodded at him to go back in. He knew that there'd be no way for his cousins to get to her safe in bed, but Kieran also didn't want her to wake alone.

"Luca," Caspar called. "Let me introduce you to Kieran Smith."

The tall dark-haired shifter strolled across the room with his hand held out. "It's nice to meet you."

Kieran sniffed but shook hands. The scent of the man was unique. Close to a wolf but not quite the same. He breathed deeply. "Coyote?"

Luca grinned. "Yes."

No wonder Dakota was utilizing Luca. He'd be a good contact to have in regards to Jeremy. "What brings you to Vegas?"

"I work for the Coalition. I'm here to transport a prisoner back to Arizona."

Kieran hated the Coalition. They weren't anything more than a bunch of shifters who cared more about gaining power than actually doing their fucking jobs. He growled.

Luca surprised him by chuckling. "Yeah, I get that reaction a lot." He waved his hand. "It's okay, I'm proud of the work I do and those that I help. I worked for the human ATF agency before. Being with the Coalition I see that I'm able to actually make a difference."

"If you say so."

"Caspar told me about Dakota. I offered my help. I'm pretty good," Luca said.

"Have you ever gone up against Walkers before?" Kieran asked.

"No."

"And you don't know the city since you're not from here," Kieran pointed out.

"Right."

"So how exactly are you going to help?" Kieran questioned point-blank.

"I'm really good at blowing things up," Luca stated.

"Uh!" Jackson lifted a hand. "I'd really appreciate it if my hotel wasn't blown up."

Luca frowned. "But…"

Fuck. Kieran laughed. He actually found this guy funny.

"Maybe just a parking garage?" Luca said hopefully.

"No," Jackson and Caspar both said.

Luca leaned closer to Kieran. "I hear that word a lot."

"Me, too," Kieran admitted.

"I don't usually listen," Luca shared.

"Me, neither," Kieran agreed.

"Oh, God!" Remy exclaimed. "There are two of them! What in the hell were you thinking, bringing Luca?"

Caspar was glancing back and forth between Kieran and Luca. "It seemed like a good idea at the time. He works with the biggest and strongest Coalition force. I thought we could use the help. I'd prefer not to wreck an entire city going after the two Walkers."

Luca winked at Kieran. "Yeah, I might not have been the best choice. But I'm here now." He walked over to Mitch and plopped down on the couch. "Besides I'd never even met one Walker and now I'm in a suite with four. This is pretty fucking cool."

Mitch flashed his fangs when Luca sat too close.

"It's okay, boy." Luca patted Mitch's leg. "I don't bite."

"But I do," Mitch threatened. "I'm working here."

"So, show me what you've got."

Kieran turned away from Luca and Mitch. Remy was still standing in the middle of the room with a shocked expression. Caspar and Jackson were staying as far from each other as possible. Oh, yeah, Kieran had forgotten they didn't like each other.

Jesus, this was a mess. His lover was passed out with some kind of poison in her and this was the group that was going to help him get his revenge? Things had been a lot easier when he'd worked by himself.

"I want to be out there hunting Marcel and Elijah," Kieran said.

"We lost them," Jackson reminded him. "Without scent, they can't be tracked. Our best bet is the security cameras and that takes time."

"They have to feed, right?" Luca asked.

"What?" Kieran gave him his attention.

"They need blood. Have there been any reports of an attack?"

Kieran glanced at Remy who rushed over to one of the open laptops on the desk. That was a good start but… "It might not be reported. We don't normally kill people. A couple of mouthfuls and we're done."

Luca shrugged. "It's worth checking out."

It was.

"Two nights ago a woman reported that she and her daughter was coming out of the Fashion Show mall and were attacked by two men. They didn't take her money. The victim claimed they must have injected her and the girl with something, because they became violently ill. The police are treating it as some kind of bio weapon," Remy informed them.

"Bio weapon my ass," Kieran commented. "That was them. How old was the girl?"

Remy read some more. "Eight."

"We don't take blood from kids. The symptoms hit them harder."

"Well, one of your cousins doesn't care," Remy stated.

Kieran nodded. "Who wants to go for a ride? I want to check out where this attack took place."

"I'll go." Luca rose.

"Me, too," Remy added.

"No," Kieran told Remy. "I want you to do me a favor."

Remy pouted. "What? I want to have some fun."

"Look for a trail from Texas to here to see how Marcel and Elijah traveled. They might have left clues in their victims. I really want to know if they make a habit of feeding from children."

Remy gave a long sigh. "Fine." He dropped down into a chair. "But if you see your cousins, you'd better call me."

"I promise," Kieran agreed. He looked up at Jackson. "You got things here?"

"I'll keep you apprised."

"What do you want from me?" Caspar asked.

Kieran glanced at him. Caspar was usually the one who gave the orders.

"I'm here to help!" Caspar stated firmly.

"Have the on-duty patrols out searching?" Kieran requested. "We have their photos now."

"I can do that."

Now that a plan had been made, Kieran felt better. Not as good as he would when he got his hands on his cousins, but this was a start.

"Call me if she wakes up," Kieran said to Jackson.

"I will. Don't worry about her."

Kieran nodded at Luca before stalking toward the door. He didn't think that he'd actually find anything, but it was worth checking out. Even when they'd been growing up, Kieran's father hadn't allowed them to take children's blood. He was really curious to see if that had changed or if his cousins were off on their own.

"Did you come with Caspar?" Kieran asked as he and Luca approached the elevator.

"No, I wasn't sure of my welcome. I rode my bike."

"Bike?" Maybe Kieran wouldn't have to drive one of their SUVs.

"You ride, don't you?"

"Yep," Kieran responded. "And I could go for a ride."

"Sounds good to me."

They stepped into the elevator and Kieran turned to the agent. "Mated?"

Luca's head snapped up. "Yes."

He nodded. "Human?"

"Is that a problem?" Luca bristled.

"Not for me," Kieran assured him. "I can just smell her on you. Pretty strongly, as a matter of fact."

Luca laughed. "I rub my undershirt on her when I have to be away. It helps calm my coyote."

"That's...a good idea." Kieran wasn't sure that was something he'd ever do, but he could see why a shifter would need it. He often wondered how much instinct Dakota held back from him.

"You can make fun of me," Luca said. He was grinning, though. "Everyone does. It's hard away being away from my family. I can't stand being away from my mate."

"And she accepts that you're a shifter?" Kieran asked. The elevator doors opened and he stepped out with Luca at his heels.

"She worked for the FBI before she joined the Coalition. She was already partnered up with a wolf shifter before we met."

"That's convenient," Kieran quipped.

"It really is." Luca shrugged. "A couple of my buddies had to explain being a shifter to their mates and it isn't always easy. How about you? How'd Dakota find out you're a Walker?"

Kieran didn't mind sharing his story, at least that part—everyone in the Organization knew, anyway. "Caspar sent me here on vacation. Then he assigned her and Dean to follow me and make sure I didn't cause any trouble. She knew what I was."

Luca slapped his back as they reached the outer door. "We're going to get along so well."

The rain had stopped, so taking their motorcycles should be fine. Kieran shook his head. He didn't want to agree, but he did already feel comfortable with this crazy coyote shifter.

Chapter Seven

There was no evidence of an attack in the parking garage of the mall but Kieran could see why his cousins had picked that location. Too many potential victims walked to and from the shopping center, paying no attention to their surroundings. He counted at least a dozen humans he could have attacked.

It was a shame that no one was really safe in the city. No matter how good a job they did in the Organization, they couldn't be everywhere.

"Yeah, I can see why they'd pick this place," Luca murmured.

Kieran glanced over. Luca had his hands in his pockets as he studied the area.

"And right here is a camera blind spot."

"They had to have staked out this place," Kieran said.

"Which means they might not be too far away," Luca agreed. "Care for a walk?"

"Yeah." He glanced around, trying to guess what direction to take. From between the concrete barriers, he spotted a building. An older hotel that stood in the shadows of the larger casinos. "Let's head that way." He motioned with his head.

Luca looked over before nodding.

The sidewalk was uneven as they circled around the back of the buildings. It would be the most direct route to the hotel he'd spotted.

Only a couple blocks away, the streets were crowded by both locals and tourists. With it still being early evening and now that the rain had stopped, he could clearly hear the chaos of the city livening up. Kieran was glad he didn't have to go out there with them.

"It would be helpful if your kind had a scent," Luca muttered. He was sniffing around while darting his gaze back and forth.

"True," Kieran conceded. "But you can also use the lack of scent as a resource."

"What do you mean?"

Kieran stopped walking. He lifted his head and pulled in the odors of the sidewalk around him. "There's a dumpster around the corner. In front of it we'll find a couple of drops of blood."

"Your awareness of scent is that strong?" Luca sounded shocked.

He didn't want to admit that his abilities were more extreme than other Walkers, so he simply nodded. Caspar had told him that he needed to embrace who he was. If it helped to track down his cousins, Kieran was going to use every bit of his heightened abilities.

"Check the area directly in front of the spot. You'll notice that there is no scent whatsoever. That's how you'll know a Walker was there. Whoever was bleeding should have left some kind of scent behind."

Luca raced off and Kieran had to jog to keep up with him. When the shifter dropped to his knees right where Kieran had noted the missing odor, Kieran grinned. It might be fun to see how much he could push his unique gifts.

"I think I get it," Luca said, glancing over his shoulder. "So they were here?"

"Maybe." Kieran didn't want to get too excited yet. "We don't know it was them. But whoever stood there was bleeding."

"That's a good sign," Luca said. "Too bad it's not enough blood to follow."

"True, but I think it means we're on the right track."

"They've been hunting here," Luca guessed.

"Let's keep going. We might come across something else."

Luca stood. Kieran let him go first so Kieran could concentrate on the areas around them. It helped having a trained shifter along with him. Luca, much like Remy, would be able to alert him in case of danger.

Kieran concentrated on picking up every sound he could pinpoint. Instead of sticking to a couple of blocks like he did when he was hunting, Kieran changed tactics.

Unsure what to do, Kieran picked a point close to the windows of the old hotel to visualize. No one could have been more shocked then him when he actually heard the voice of the taxi driver who had pulled up in front of the building and was speaking to his fare. *Holy shit!* Kieran was doing it.

He sped up but kept his gaze on his target. If he could just overhear one of his cousins talking, he would know where they were. *This was great.*

Luca ran beside him as Kieran used his Walker speed to reach his destination. He stopped across an alley and stayed hidden behind a bundle of trash.

"Did you see something?" Luca asked. He was panting but seemed in good enough shape to continue.

Kieran shook his head, not wanting to pull his attention from his task.

The cement structure should have been a barrier to keep Kieran from having the ability to hear through walls. Instead, he began at the first floor where the reception area be. Two employees were discussing a woman and a much older man who'd rented a room. The employees were speculating that she was a prostitute.

"Okay, I'll keep watch. You just do whatever it is you're doing," Luca whispered.

Kieran moved farther across the floor. Once he was certain his cousins were downstairs, he moved to the next level, eavesdropping on room after room.

Luckily, the building wasn't that big.

It had probably been built in the fifties or sixties. Unlike the large hotel and casino combinations, this place was geared more to people down on their luck, or locals. Kieran wouldn't have looked for his cousins in a place like this. Not with the money that his family had.

His cell rang. Damn it, he had to pull his attention away as he dug into the front pocket of his jeans.

"Hello?"

"Where are you?" Mitch asked.

Kieran searched until he found the address. "1514 McAdams."

"Oh." Mitch sounded disappointed. "Did you find them?"

"Not yet. Why?"

"I caught an image of both men going into that hotel. It's just a blur as they were using this supernatural speed, but I got it. They went to that address."

That confirmed his hunch. "Get Remy, Jackson, Caspar and anyone else who can get here. I'm on the corner across from the alley. I'll narrow down where they are. We're going in."

"You got it." Mitch disconnected the call.

Kieran shoved the device back in his pocket and glanced at Luca. "You heard all that?"

"Yeah," Luca whispered. "How are you going to find them?"

"Just give me a minute." Kieran narrowed his eyes and went back to the middle of the fourth floor where he'd been scanning. Two windows later, he heard what he needed.

"Hurry," Marcel demanded. "We need to get out of here."

"I'm packing as fast as I can," Elijah whined. "I said that we weren't ready to make a move. If we'd have waited, we wouldn't have had to come back here."

"It was too good a moment. Fuck, I would have loved to see the look on Kieran's face when he realized it was us," Marcel said.

Elijah laughed. "Yeah, me, too. I can't believe he's fucking a shifter. I can't wait to tell our father."

"We'll call him after we relocate," Marcel stated.

"I'm ready."

"Fuck," Kieran spat. He nudged Luca. "They're on the way out."

Luca was frowning. "That's sort of creepy."

Kieran smirked. "Take the right side of the door and I'll take the left. Hopefully, the others will get here soon."

"All right." Luca sprinted across the alley. Kieran made sure Luca was safely in the shadows before dashing to the end of the building. Kieran was merely guessing in what direction his cousins would go. He didn't think they'd want to be caught on the Strip.

After pressing his back to the side of the building, he attempted to pick up his cousins' conversation again. Either they weren't talking, or Kieran wasn't doing it right. He heard several people talking, but not the ones he wanted.

Disappointed, he tried to sense if his team was coming. *Nothing. Damn it.*

Kieran peeked around the corner, but no one was on the street. He couldn't even see Luca, although he knew the coyote shifter was there.

"Come on," he murmured. He was ready to make the two men who'd dared to hurt his lover pay.

He heard Elijah even as the outer door swung open. Kieran darted back out of sight, hoping he'd picked the correct direction they'd go. *Yes!* Elijah's voice became clearer as he bitched about losing the money for their night's stay.

Kieran rolled his eyes. He knew how much money both men had.

"Shut up," Marcel snapped. "We knew this was possible. This is why we set up secondary locations."

"I just think—"

Kieran stepped around the corner a few feet from them.

Marcel halted, but Elijah took another couple of steps before realizing someone stood in front of him.

"I got your message," Kieran spat. "Now I have one for you." The identical looks of shock on their faces would be a sight that Kieran always remembered.

"Cousin," Marcel greeted, recovering first.

Kieran bared his fangs. "You attacked my lover."

"Imagine our surprise when we found out that little tidbit," Marcel replied.

Luca should be moving in from behind. He just needed to keep both his cousins' attention on him. "It was none of your business. What are you doing here?"

"Isn't it obvious?" Marcel strode forward, putting Elijah behind him. Marcel always did have one weakness. His younger brother. "We're here to see you."

"You could have called," Kieran said.

"That wouldn't have been any fun," Marcel quipped.

"Is there anything you need to say before I fuck you up?" Kieran asked. He really did want to know what they wanted.

"Yeah, right." Elijah spoke to him for the first time. "You always were a pussy. Now that we see the life of luxury you live, we know things haven't changed."

Kieran snorted. "You're one to talk. Have you even moved out of your childhood bedroom or are you still sucking on your mama's tit?"

Elijah growled and stepped forward, but Marcel put his arm up to block him.

"You'll pay for that comment," Marcel stated.

Kieran widened his stance. Marcel would attack soon and Kieran hoped Luca would have Elijah covered. "You'll pay for a lot. Everything that you've done since you've entered my city. You don't belong here."

Marcel launched himself at Kieran, trying to take him by surprise, but Kieran was ready. He allowed Marcel's momentum to carry him forward.

Kieran caught him with a punch to the throat. Marcel grunted as he dropped while Elijah roared. Luca came out of the shadows and leapt at Elijah's back, taking him down. Kieran jumped on top of Marcel, slamming his fist into his cousin's face.

Blood erupted around him, but he easily ignored the scent. This was for Dakota.

He took a hard strike to the ribs, probably breaking a few, and rolled onto his knees. Marcel attempted to crawl away, but Kieran kicked his knee before grabbing hold of his shoulder.

Behind him, he heard the roar of a pissed-off coyote and even more blood flowed. *Shit.* Kieran couldn't worry about Luca. He had his hands full with Marcel. Where they hell were the rest of his guys? A shifter was no match for a Walker and Luca was going to need help.

Marcel pulled a knife out from somewhere and Kieran had to doge a couple of swipes before one cut his forearm. He hissed, ignoring the pain, and yanked harder on Marcel's arm. There was a *pop*, Marcel's shoulder dislocating, before Kieran was tackled.

He tucked his chin to avoid an injury to his vulnerable neck.

"Come on!" Elijah pulled up a bloody and beaten Marcel.

Kieran sprung at them. Elijah lifted his foot and kicked him in the face. Pain exploded and he grabbed his nose, which was broken. Kieran blinked away the tears, but Marcel and Elijah were already running. He leapt up to his feet, glancing behind him.

"Fuck!" Kieran changed direction, to drop beside Luca who had a dagger in his leg and was bleeding badly from the neck. Shit, it looked like Elijah had taken a chunk out of him.

"I...I'm okay," Luca panted. "Go after them."

He couldn't, though. There was no way he'd leave Luca behind with such serious injuries. Kieran ripped off his shirt and pressed it to Luca's neck wound. "Hang on, buddy."

Running caught his attention and he looked up in time to see Jackson reaching him. Mitch wasn't too far behind.

"They took off that way!" Kieran pointed.

Jackson nodded before both Walkers continued on. Remy was sprinting toward him. As soon as his partner reached him, Kieran pointed to the knife in Luca's leg.

"Got it. Caspar's right behind me with the SUV. We'll get him back to the suite."

"He's losing a lot of blood," Kieran yelled. Damn it, he should have waited, or just followed his cousins. Luca wouldn't have gotten hurt.

"Let me see." Remy shoved his hands off the shirt before lifting the edge. "He's already healing. It'll be fine."

"Good." Kieran let out a breath of relief.

A black SUV screeched to a stop beside them, blocking off the alley.

"You okay?" Caspar asked, skirting around the vehicle.

"Yeah. Luca's not."

Caspar fell to his knees, allowing Kieran to move back to give his boss room to work. He turned his head when he sensed Jackson coming back.

"They're gone," Jackson declared. He wasn't even winded.

Kieran nodded, since he'd expected as much. "They left behind all their belongings," he said, motioning with his head. "That's gonna hurt."

"From the amount of blood on the ground, I'd say you did a little damage yourself," Jackson praised.

Kieran grinned. "Oh, yeah, they'll be moving slower, for sure."

"We need to go!" Caspar called.

"Mitch and I will pick up their stuff. You help Caspar get Luca back."

"Thanks." Kieran glanced over his shoulder back toward where Marcel and Elijah had disappeared. They might have gotten away, but Kieran would hunt them down. It was time he cleaned the trash from his city.

* * * *

Dakota's head was pounding and her limbs felt so heavy. She didn't know what had happened, but she regretted whatever she'd done. She moaned, trying to blink open her eyes.

"That's it. Wake up for me." Kieran's voice sounded warm and gentle. His chest moved as he spoke. She must be lying on him.

She rubbed her cheek against him before finally finding the energy to open her eyes.

"Hi." Kieran ran his thumb over her cheekbone.

"What the fuck?" she croaked. His entire face was bruised. Two black eyes and his nose had been broken.

Kieran chuckled. "I'll be completely healed in a couple of hours."

That was true. He wouldn't even have the black eyes later. "What happened?"

"Do you remember what happened downstairs?"

"I was attacked," she recalled.

"My cousins," Kieran admitted.

Oh, wow! That's unexpected. "Your cousins?"

"Yeah, Marcel and Elijah."

"Is that who tried to rearrange your face?" she questioned.

"I gave better than I got," he said with pride.

She reached up, carefully tracing his lips. "At least I can still kiss you."

He lowered his mouth and gave her a very soft, sweet kiss. He tried to pull away, but she whined while pushing up for more. After she'd gotten a good taste of her man, she let him go.

"How're you feeling?"

Dakota had to think about her answer. "Like I'd gotten drunk then run over by a car. I shouldn't have been hurt so bad by bumping into a wall." She couldn't make sense of it.

"First, you were thrown into the wall so hard there a dent. Second, you were injected with some sort of poison."

"I was *poisoned*?"

Kieran clenched his jaw.

"But I'm okay, right? Nothing permanent?"

"Now that you've woken up, you should be fine. Might feel sick and weak for a while."

"Did you catch them?" She hoped Kieran had not only kicked their asses but that both men were sitting in one of their cells.

"No, they got away. But we found them once—we'll do it again."

"Damn." Dakota tried to sit up. "What do we need to do? Any leads?"

"What do you think you're doing?" Kieran barked.

She turned her head, frowning at him. "Getting up, so we can get to work."

"Lie down," he grumbled. He pressed on her neck. Since she didn't have the energy to fight him, she complied.

"Mitch and Dean are working on finding them. Jackson, Alex and the security here are going over this entire building to make sure we don't have any weak spots. And Caspar is watching over Luca."

"What happened to Luca?" she asked. "Wait, you know who Luca is?"

Kieran chuckled. "Yes, I met him. Caspar brought him over after you were attacked. He went with me after my cousins and was hurt."

"Fuck." She groaned.

"He'll be all right. He's pissed that Elijah got the better of him. Already Luca swears he'll be the one to take Elijah down."

"That sounds like something he'd say," Dakota mused. "I was going to have you meet him."

"I heard." Kieran peered down at her. "You liked him. Thought that I should get to know him."

"Yeah. He's not like the other shifters."

"So he's not an asshole?"

She weakly slapped at him. "He probably is, but he's not afraid of you. He actually asked to meet you. Something to do with you saving a family a couple of years ago."

"He didn't mention it, but we were kind of busy," Kieran said. "I'll ask him about it later."

"Good." Since Kieran wasn't allowing her up, Dakota was just going to enjoy the cuddling. She ran her fingers over the thin Henley covering Kieran's chest. This couldn't be easy for him. And she didn't even know the whole story. "Do you want to talk about it?"

She didn't press when Kieran remained silent. One thing she'd learned about her lover was that he'd talk when he was ready and not before. He held a lot in. Dakota didn't know if that was how he'd always been or if his behavior was a result of the years of torture.

Her eyes were drifting closed when he cleared his throat.

"I never fit in," he explained. "Not from the time I could remember. My father is a powerful businessman. All he cared about was making money and gaining power for the family. It was all about appearances and for some reason I didn't measure up. I used to listen to him and my mom argue about me. My dad blamed her for babying me."

"And your sisters?"

"They spent most of their times hanging out with friends and shopping. They had each other. As the only boy I wasn't included."

"So you had no one?"

"My cousins were there quite a bit. My uncle is exactly like my father and they always ganged up on me. We got into a lot of fights. My father always took their side and once they left, I'd get in trouble for not getting along with them."

"That's not fair."

Kieran grunted. "That's just how it was. When my father sent me away at eighteen, I begged him to allow me to stay. I didn't understand why I had to live on my own when no one else ever had. He told me that the only way I'd ever become a man was if I had no other choice."

"You've talked about this before. How he just sent you away," she whispered. It still broke her heart to think about how scared Kieran must have been.

"When he gave me the money and keys to one of our vehicles, I thought he was testing me. But then he turned his back. Didn't say another word to me. I haven't seen him since. I never even considered going home after I was rescued. I knew he'd only blame me for being captured by the shifters. I'd proven to him that I was as weak as he'd always claimed."

Dakota rolled so she covered his lower body and could look up at him. "You're not weak."

"I know, or at least I know that now. And it's no thanks to him. Caspar brought me into his home and built me up, trained me and showed me that not everyone expected me to fail."

"He brought you into the Organization."

"And introduced me to Remy and Angel. They were the first people who I ever trusted to have my back." He ran his hands through her hair. "Then he sent me here and I met you."

She grinned. "Pretty lucky."

Kieran snorted. "Yeah, I am. I don't know who I would have ended up being if things had gone differently. If I'd stayed home, not been kidnapped or joined the Organization, I might have been exactly like my cousins."

"No," she murmured. "You wouldn't have."

"Why not? Aren't they a product of their upbringing?"

"Perhaps," she conceded. "But someone's heart won't lie. You can't hide who you are, Kieran. And that's a hero, the good guy."

"You know I've killed people. That I have no problems killing. I actually enjoy it."

Oh, yeah, he'd never hid that from her. "Have you ever hurt or killed someone who didn't deserve it? Ever gone after an innocent?"

He didn't respond.

"Yes, Kieran, I know. I'm okay with that."

"I love you." He spoke the words quietly but this time kept his eyes on hers. "I want to be a better man for you."

"I don't need a better man. I just want you."

"Caspar said I needed to embrace who I am, what was done to me," he confessed.

She hated to see the worry in his gaze or the lines in his forehead. "It's good advice."

"And if I become the monster that I've been trying to fight all this time?"

"You won't." Dakota was certain.

"How do you know?"

"Because I'd never allow it. You think I'll let you go now that I have you? No way. You belong to me," she declared.

"I do, do I?"

"One hundred percent. You'd better not forget it either."

"I won't." He cupped her face. "You need to—"

A knock on the bedroom door interrupted what Kieran had started to say.

"Come in!" Kieran called.

"Jackson's back." Remy poked his head in. "Oh, hey! You're awake."

Dakota grinned at the wolf shifter. "Yep."

"Good. How're you feeling?"

"Better," Dakota said. Kieran was right about her being tired, but Dakota had felt worse.

"Glad to hear it." He glanced at Kieran. "You want to come out so we can decide what to do next?"

"I'll be right there," Kieran answered. "Why don't you order some dinner for everyone? Get Dakota some soup, please."

"Will do," Remy agreed, before backing out and closing the door behind him.

"I'm coming out there with you," Dakota wowed.

"If I thought I could keep you in bed any longer, I'd do it. I know how stubborn you are."

Dakota laughed. "I have to be, to put up with you."

"But you're lying down on the couch and listening. You're not to exert yourself."

"Promise." Dakota opened her mouth while reaching for him then hesitated.

"What is it?"

"I have to admit something to you," she admitted. "I don't know how you're going to take it." Dakota didn't want anything to hang over them.

"Go ahead," Kieran said. "I can't promise to react one way or another. You can punch me if you think I need it."

"Punch you in the throat?" she asked. It was a threat she used often but never followed through with.

"Yes, if I piss you off you can punch me in the throat.

"I just don't want you mad. Or to doubt my feelings for you."

"Did you fuck the coyote shifter?"

Dakota stood slowly. Kieran's eyes were wide as he watched her. Had he just fucking asked that? *Oh, hell, no!* She reared back and punched him in the throat. Just like she'd said she would.

He dropped. Straight down to his knees while wheezing.

"You asshole!"

Kieran was waving his hands to ward her off.

"I ought to kick you in the balls, too!"

He desperately shook his head.

Dakota sat on the side of the mattress as she waited for him to recover. Well, she wasn't nervous anymore. Now she was just pissed off.

Eventually Kieran glanced up with tears trailing down his cheeks. "Sorry," he croaked. "I don't know why I said that."

"Hmm."

"Baby, please. I'm sorry."

He looked so pitiful, kneeling. She sighed. "I thought your cousin was good-looking. In the hallway, before he attacked. Not better than you, but similar. I didn't see the resemblance right away, but I can now."

"That's it?"

Dakota nodded.

"Oh, well…" Kieran shrugged. "Okay."

"I just wanted to tell you. Even if I'd been single, it's not something I would have acted on."

"But you can appreciate a good-looking man," Kieran said. "I'm crazy, but I'm not a possessive asshole."

She lifted a brow.

"Okay," Kieran said. "Asshole, yes. But I haven't ever cared if you looked at someone else. I know whose bed you'll end up in."

"Do you? Because now I'm questioning it."

"Don't," Kieran pleaded. He walked on his knees to her. "I don't doubt you, so don't doubt me. My mouth runs away sometimes. You know this."

She did. Maybe he hadn't meant it, but there was more to this insecurity then she'd thought. Dakota would have liked to talk more about it, but there was a room full of people next door.

"Let me help you get dressed," Kieran said.

"Okay, for now."

He smiled over his shoulder before walking to the dresser. Kieran pulled out her favorite pair of pajama bottoms and a soft, faded T-shirt.

Dakota let him dress her but squawked when he lifted her into his arms. "I can walk."

"Maybe I just like carrying you."

"Well, I'm not helpless. Put me down," she ordered.

Kieran, of course, ignored her. He opened the door and strolled out into the main room without saying a word.

Jackson, Alex, Caspar and Remy were all sitting at the table across the room. Luca was slouched in one of the chairs and smiled when he saw her. Kieran stomped to the couch then gingerly set her down. He grabbed the blanket off the back and tucked it around her. Dakota rolled her eyes but let him fuss. Once he was done, she lifted an eyebrow.

"Shut up," he muttered.

"Glad to see you in one piece," Luca greeted her.

Kieran crossed the room before looking over at the coyote shifter. He grunted but didn't comment to the agent.

"You, too. Heard you went up against a Walker," she teased.

Luca scowled. "I held my own. At least for a few minutes." He smiled, wide and bright. "Next time, I'll be more prepared."

"Well, you did want to meet one," Dakota pointed out.

"Yeah, but not exactly how I was thinking. I should be more specific next time."

"Probably a good idea," Dakota said. "How're you feeling?"

Luca touched the side of his neck. "I won't even have a scar to tell my mate about by the time I get home."

"Aww," she teased. "That would have totally gotten you laid."

"I know!" Luca threw his hands up.

They both laughed. "Thanks for having his back," she said quietly. No doubt that if anyone else was listening they'd hear, but Dakota didn't care.

"It was actually pretty cool. You know, before someone tried to take my head off my shoulders. I've never worked with a Walker before. He's fast and I swear he was listening to the inside of the building. I didn't even know that was possible."

Dakota hadn't, either, but she suspected only Kieran would manage it. She really did need to find out the details on what Kieran could do. Before, he hadn't wanted to talk about it, but hopefully now he'd be more willing.

"I was supposed be heading back tomorrow, but I called my boss and he's letting me stay. I can help with this as well as with Jeremy and the other kids."

"I'm glad to hear it," Dakota said. "Jeremy seemed to be doing better after he spoke to you."

"He's a good kid," Luca said. "I was going to talk to you about him."

"Oh, yeah?"

"I called my parents and told them about Jeremy, Adam and Carmen. Now that their kids have moved out and away, they don't even get to see their grandkids that much. We have plenty of room and I think they'd make good foster parents for shifters."

"Really?" Dakota started to sit up, but Kieran turned to her with a scowl. "Sorry." She lay back down. "Your Pack would let a wolf and bobcat in the territory as well?"

"Coyotes are different from wolves. We live in Packs, but ours are made up differently. A coyote Pack is their family. It was my mom, dad and siblings. Now the grandchildren. But they don't share territory with other families. That's why the Packs are so much smaller. As foster kids, the teens would be part of the Pack, my family."

Dakota couldn't believe it. "I don't know what to say. I'd hoped you'd have some ideas on where he could go, but I hadn't thought your family would take him."

"I believe it'll be best for everyone. My dad will love helping them grow into their powers and my mom needs someone to fret over."

"That sounds like heaven," Dakota mused. "That'd be so happy staying together."

"Adam is good for Jeremy. He acts like his big brother, protective and defensive, of him. Carmen is like their little sister. With her, Jeremy gets to be the defender," Luca said.

"The food should be here any minute." Kieran joined them. He sat beside Dakota before eyeing Luca.

Luca lifted his hands. "I'm really am fine. Stop worrying."

"I should have been more careful."

"I knew what I was getting into."

Kieran frowned.

"Okay, maybe not so much of what going up against a Walker. I need to know how to handle them, though.

What happens if I'm working and come across a Walker?"

"I haven't thought about that," Kieran said.

"There's not a lot of information out there about your kind. And I understand why. I'll actually keep what I learn to myself and the agents who work with me."

"We'd appreciate it," Kieran said. He nodded toward Jackson and Mitch. "For the most part, Day Walkers keep to themselves. But we've noticed more and more coming out and causing trouble. Jackson keeps a close eye on this city. Out where you are, I have no idea how many of our kind is there."

"I understand. So what are we going to be doing about your cousins?" Luca asked.

"We've agreed that we'll keep searching for them, but they'll be coming for me. They're here for a reason. They made it a point to go after Dakota when they could've just approached me."

"Which means they're not here to reconnect," Luca guessed.

"No, they aren't," Kieran agreed. "So we'll let them get to me."

"Excuse me!" Dakota interrupted. "I don't think so."

Kieran gripped her hand. "Just listen."

"Listen as you use yourself as bait for two crazed men who have no problem hurting or killing you? I don't think so."

"He won't actually be alone," Jackson said, joining them. "I'll be with him, even when he and Remy are on patrol. Caspar had agreed to let me shadow them."

"Yeah, but that doesn't mean—"

"This is the best we can come up with," Kieran said. "We'll still be looking for them, but I honestly believe if we let them, they'll come to me."

"If anything happens to you, I'm going to be mad," Dakota warned.

"I understand. Which brings up something I need to talk to you about."

"What?" If he was going to tell her she needed to stay home or not work, she'd hit him.

"Alex will be tailing you," Kieran said.

"No."

"He'll do the same as Jackson, where he'll work in the shadows. You won't even know he's there."

"No," she repeated.

"They already went after you once," Kieran argued.

"And they won't try it again. They made their point. They can get to me."

"He's still going to be with you. This isn't up for discussion."

Oh, the hell it isn't. "He would be more valuable looking for your cousins instead of looking after me."

"Doesn't matter." The look on his face told her she was in for a fight. Dakota would let the subject go for now, only because she was tired, but they would talk about it later. When Kieran didn't have help trying to convince her.

"Food's coming," Kieran stated. He leaned over and kissed her before rising.

Dakota watched him walk toward the door. Her man had one spectacular ass. She wanted to sink her teeth into his taunt muscles.

He glanced over her shoulder and winked. Dakota ducked her head at getting caught ogling him.

Chapter Eight

Dakota choose her favorite pair of jeans as well as a black V-neck T-shirt to wear for the day. Kieran's gaze hadn't left her since she'd woken up. He hadn't said anything about her going into the office and she was glad. Dakota did not want to fight with him and, if Kieran insisted on her staying home, she wouldn't be able to let his overprotectiveness pass. Not that she didn't understand his concern — she still felt a little worn. Nothing she couldn't handle, though.

"Do you want breakfast?" he asked. Kieran had dressed in his customary jeans and Henley. He looked like a tall and muscular Greek God.

"I want a kiss."

He brightened. "Yeah?"

She finished tying her boots then motioned him closer. "Come here." As soon as he was close enough, Dakota grabbed the front of his shirt and yanked him forward.

Kieran was laughing when their lips touched. Once she'd gotten her wish, Dakota allowed Kieran to pull her up.

"So, breakfast?" Kieran asked. "I'm thinking we could stop in the café downstairs."

"Really?" They rarely ate in the café. Kieran preferred avoiding the crowds and ordering room service or getting something on the go.

"We have time."

"And you want to be out in the open."

"Maybe I just want to make sure you eat properly," he countered.

Dakota laughed while shaking her head but strolled out of the bedroom to gather her bag. "It's fine with me."

Kieran caught her by the hem of her shirt, yanking her back.

"What?"

"Thank you." He lowered his head before running his tongue over her bottom lip. "I know you don't like what I'm doing."

"I've thought a lot about it overnight," Dakota admitted. She'd only managed to sleep off and on. Every time she'd closed her eyes, Dakota had seen the faces of the two men who had attacked her. It wasn't what they'd done to her, though, that was troubling. Marcel and Elijah Argent had tormented Kieran. After dinner, Kieran had given her the file that the Organization had collected on his family. She'd been interested in seeing more on Kieran's parents, but now she wished she hadn't read it. "I'll support you. I just want you to be careful."

"I will," Kieran promised. "I'm not going to let them hurt anyone else, though, if they can't get to me."

"Let's do this, then," she told him. "But once we have your cousins taken care of, we're going to talk about taking that vacation."

"Sounds good to me."

It didn't take them long to be out of the suite and into the elevator. Mitch was planning on working in their suite during the day so he'd be on location, but also guaranteeing that no one got inside their place. It had been Alex's idea and, Dakota had to admit, it was a good one.

"I take it we have our shadows?" Dakota asked as they rode downstairs.

"Yes," Kieran answered. "Jackson texted me."

She'd finally consented to being followed – the only reason being if she hadn't, Kieran would be worried about her. Dakota didn't want to be the reason that Kieran let his guard down. It had taken Caspar explaining how Kieran would worry if she didn't allow Alex to watch over her to make her understand. "Good. You're buying me a latte and a muffin."

He grinned.

The door opened. Kieran stuck his head out to check the area before motioning Dakota forward. She strolled out confidently in case anyone was watching. A small hallway left from the elevator. To the left stood the door they'd take to the parking garage, but to the right was the main floor of the casino.

Kieran slipped his hand into hers.

It being late afternoon, the main floor was crowded and loud. Even though Kieran wasn't fond of the mass of people, Dakota enjoyed watching the unique assembly of the crowd. This was what Vegas was all about, after all. Being able to let one's hair down and have fun. She might not want to take her vacation there, but she understood why others did. It was her job to make sure the tourists were safe while doing so.

"Of course, there's a line," Kieran bitched under his breath.

Dakota chuckled. She led Kieran to the line, trying to ignore Alex sitting in the corner with a large cup in front of him. Jackson seemed certain that neither Marcel nor Elijah had seen him before. That was what made him safe to tail Dakota.

The baristas were well trained and, even though they were busy, the line moved quickly.

Dakota ordered a large black coffee for Kieran and a large vanilla latte for herself. She also got him a breakfast sandwich and her a cranberry orange muffin. Handing over a twenty, she winked at the cute college-age guy taking her order, telling him to keep the change. Kieran snorted but didn't reply. As they waited, Kieran slid his arm around her shoulders, pulling her close. Dakota would love it to have been because he couldn't keep his hands off her, but she knew he was checking out the area around them. That was okay. When she did get him alone, away from town and without threats, she'd get a little public display of affection.

"Here you go!" the barista called.

Dakota accepted their tray, but Kieran took it from her before leading her to the opposite side of the café from Alex. Once seated, Dakota placed Kieran's food and coffee in front of him before picking up her own latte. She took a deep sniff of her flavored brew just to enjoy.

"What are your plans once you get to the office?" Kieran asked.

Since he already knew, Dakota assumed the conversation was for the benefit of anyone who was listening. "I'll check in on the kids and see if Luca heard back from his parents. His mom wanted to talk over the decision with the rest of the family."

Kieran gave her a real smile. "I can't believe how well that situation might turn out. That's going to be a real break for the kids. Do you think they'll accept?"

"I do," Dakota answered after sipping her coffee. "It's the best thing for Jeremy so Adam and Carmen will agree. If Jeremy understands the chance he's being offered, he'll be excited."

"It'll be good for him to finally be around people like him," Kieran said.

Even though shifters were out to the public, Kieran was being careful with his words. Dakota found it funny that her lover refused to talk about anything paranormal out loud.

They finished their food quickly and Dakota cleaned the table before guiding the way out of the café.

"You riding in?" she asked. Dakota hated the idea that he'd be vulnerable on the way to the office.

"Yeah. I might need my bike later."

Or he wanted to give Marcela and Elijah a chance to get at him. She stopped at the glass door to pull him into a kiss. "Be careful."

"You, too."

They separated at the curb and Dakota didn't waste any time getting to her SUV. She didn't want to be too far behind him. She climbed into her vehicle before locking the door. Dakota examined the immediate area but didn't sense anyone else around.

Slowly, she put the key into the ignition and started the engine. Dakota carefully backed out of her spot and drove to the exit. Kieran's bike was already gone. She pressed down on the gas pedal, pulling out into traffic.

"Please be okay," she murmured.

Being alone for the first time since she'd woken up the previous evening gave Dakota a chance to just take in everything that had happened in the past twenty-four hours. It also gave her time to think about her own family.

Dakota might not have ever been loved, but she hadn't been mistreated.

Kieran's parents had mentally abused him while his father had shunned every bit of love Kieran tried to give him. Dakota's family had kept their distance from her, knowing that she'd have to fulfill the blood vow to the Organization. Neither of them had the childhoods they should have had, but both had come out on top.

She was pretty damn proud of them and the family they'd cobbled together.

Halfway to the office, Dakota noticed the same dark sedan from the day before. There was no way that was a coincidence. She pushed the Bluetooth button on the steering wheel.

"Call Mitch."

Calling Mitch, the mechanical voice responded.

"Hello?"

"Hey, it's Dakota," she said. "Are you logged in to the city's traffic cams?"

"I don't know what you're talking about," Mitch replied.

"I'm not going to arrest you," she said.

"As you're calling from an unsecured line, I still will not answer that question."

Damn, paranoid much? Instead of saying that, she grunted. "Well, if you were, maybe you could take a look at the corner of Forth and Falcon? I'm about to stop at a light. Two cars back is a dark sedan. I can't see the license plate."

"Anything in particular wrong with this vehicle?" Mitch questioned.

"I'm pretty sure that it also followed me to work yesterday. I shrugged it off before, but now…it seems weird."

"I'll pass along your concern and see what I'm advised to do," Mitch commented.

Since she could hear his fingers flying across his keyboard, she knew he was on his task. She was going to have to get with Jackson about Mitch's level of mistrust later, though.

"Let me know what you find," she said. Dakota hit the button to disconnect the call. The red light turned green and she drove forward. Would Marcel and Elijah be stupid enough to go after her again? They had to know if anything else happened to her, Kieran would kill them.

She was never happier having such a short drive. Dakota pulled up to the guard house, relieved that Charlie was on duty. Kieran had spent his first several months antagonizing the young man. Instead of making a complaint against Kieran, Charlie had used each prank played on him as a training tool. The talk around the office still included how Charlie was moving himself up the ranks and would be put into field work education soon. Charlie had even gained Kieran's respect, which wasn't easy.

"Hey, Charlie," Dakota greeted.

"Agent." Dakota nodded. "I heard you might be bringing company with you?"

"Huh?"

"I just received a call from someone who said they were a friend. Wanted me to know to watch out for other vehicles behind you," Charlie explained.

Dakota laughed. *Fucking Mitch.* "Yeah. I might have picked up a tail."

"Kieran already came through. Told me to keep my eyes open. I guess something bigger than just him messing with me is going on?"

"Yes," Dakota admitted. "And some people don't care who they hurt, if you know what I mean."

"I understand," Charlie said. "I'll call Caspar about doubling up out here."

"Good idea."

"You better go. I don't want your boyfriend thinking I'm flirting with you or anything."

She laughed. "No, we wouldn't want that."

Dakota waved before driving forward. She parked next to Kieran's bike, unsurprised that he was leaning against it. He had her door open once she had the engine turned off.

"You think you were followed?" he asked.

Damn, Mitch has been busy. "I don't know. That's why I called Mitch. I just find it weird that the same vehicle stayed behind me two days in a row. It'd be different if I left at the same time every day, but I'm hours later than I was yesterday."

"Why didn't you say anything to me?" Kieran shook his head. "Never mind. I'm just worried. It makes me sound like an asshole."

"Hey!" She moved up on her tiptoes. "You are an asshole."

"Thanks."

"But you're my asshole," she said.

"You bet your ass!" He gave her a hard slap, causing her to squeak.

"Let's get inside," she said. Once they were in the building, Kieran could calm down while she went to check on the teens. Hopefully, Luca had good news for her.

Kieran walked directly behind her, covering her body from the view of the street. She pulled open the stairs door, relieved when the cool air poured out. That meant safety to her.

* * * *

Kieran had said goodbye to Dakota at the medical wing before going in search of his partner. He'd already spoken on the phone to Remy. Caspar should have been in earlier than any of them.

"K!" Remy called from next to the elevator.

"There you are." Kieran jogged up to his partner. "Did you get with Caspar?"

"Yeah, he's not happy but he's sending us out on patrol. He'll monitor while giving Jackson and Mitch updates on our locations."

"Sounds good." Kieran rubbed his hands together. He was anxious to get started. "Where're we heading to?"

"Mitch suggested staying on the back side of the Strip. That's most likely where they are. We want them to know that we're looking for them. It'd be unusual if not," Remy said.

"Fine, let's go." Kieran bounced on his toes.

"This isn't Christmas morning," Remy complained. "We're going after dangerous men. You saw what they did to Luca."

"Which is why I'm anxious. I don't want anyone else targeted because they can't find me."

"Fine." Remy spun around to the elevator.

"We can take the stairs."

But the doors opened and Remy stepped inside. Kieran stomped along to join his partner. As they traveled down, Remy was texting. Kieran ignored the wolf shifter in favor of watching the floors pass.

Once the *ding* sounded, announcing their arrival, Kieran blocked Remy from exiting. He gazed out, making sure the coast was clear before waving to Remy.

"I'll drive," Remy stated.

Kieran normally took the passenger seat in the company SUVs, but tonight was different. He opened his mouth to argue, but Remy held up a hand.

"I don't want you to jump out of the vehicle while driving."

I did that one time! It was years ago, but Remy still holds that against me. "You crashed into a tree. You were fine."

"I could have been killed!" Remy argued. "And I'm driving."

"Whatever." They didn't have time to argue.

Remy hit the alarm on a key fob. Kieran followed the sound to large black truck parked several spots from where Dakota had parked earlier.

"Where'd we get this one?" Kieran asked, walking up to the truck. If he'd known this what the vehicle they'd be taking, he would have argued with Remy more.

"It's the newest acquisition. Caspar gave me the keys this morning. He says this baby comes fully loaded. We'll be connected to everyone else."

"Nice," Kieran commented after opening the door. Black leather seats in addition to a dash covered in all kind of gadgets. Mitch would bust a nut if he saw this.

"Oh, yeah!" Remy exclaimed. "This is going to fun!"

Kieran climbed into his seat and adjusted it for his long legs before looking over the console. Remy followed his lead. They were both acting like little kids, but the interior of this ride was sweet.

"Let's see how she drives," Remy stated.

"You know Dakota would punch you for naming the truck a woman."

Remy ran his hands gently over the steering wheel. "It'd be so worth it." He put the key in the ignition then turned it. The big beautiful truck roared to life. Remy practically squealed as Kieran laughed.

Then Remy was driving out of the garage way too fast. Kieran saw Charlie and another unit frowning at them as they sped away. Yeah, Caspar was probably going to hear about this. Still, his boss should know better to give them toys like this.

"Please do not forget I'm monitoring."

Kieran jumped. Remy barked out a sharp laugh. "I did tell you we're connected," Remy said.

"Uh, hey, boss," Kieran said to Caspar.

"This vehicle is brand-new. It there is even a scratch on it, I'll take it out of your ass."

Oh, that's too good a comment to let pass.

"Not a word, Kieran," Caspar said quickly.

Damn it. Kieran crossed his arms with a pout.

"I'm bringing in Mitch and Jackson online. Be careful out there," Caspar ordered.

"Yes, sir," Remy and Kieran said in union.

"Still so cool," Remy whispered. Kieran merely nodded. He didn't think that Caspar had video connected, but he wouldn't put it past his boss.

"Let's start on the opposite end from my hotel," Kieran suggested. "We can make our way over. I think they'd stay close, but not too close."

"You got it." Remy took the next right. It was time to get to work.

Kieran cracked his window. It would help not only his ability to hear, but his scent and vision. Kieran was interested to see just how much he could push his abilities. He'd been devastated to learn that his DNA had been messed with by the mad scientist who'd loved to torture him. For too long, he'd tried to avoid even thinking about what made him different. Having his cousins there, for whatever reason, Kieran was rethinking power.

"Have you fed, Kieran?"

"Damn it," Kieran snarled. "A little warning next time, Jackson."

"Did you see him jump?" Mitch laughed. "That was awesome."

Okay, so there are cameras inside. That answers one question. "Shut up, Mitch," Kieran grumbled.

"Have you?" Jackson repeated.

"Not yet," Kieran admitted. "I'm good."

"You know how stress can affect you. If you get the chance, take it," Jackson scolded.

"Yes, Dad," Kieran quipped.

"I'll knock you upside your damn head," Jackson threatened.

Since he didn't know where the cameras were, Kieran just held up his middle finger.

"Mature," Caspar commented. "This is what I miss by not being in the field any longer."

"Yeah, now you're getting fat behind your desk, old man," Kieran teased.

"Boy!" Caspar snapped. "I control what assignments you are assigned, don't forget."

"Sorry, sir." Kieran snapped out a salute.

"I don't know how you put up with him," Jackson said to Casper, no doubt.

"I sometimes wonder if it's worth it," Caspar agreed.

"Excuse me," Kieran said. "We're trying to work here."

"But this is fun!" Mitch complained.

"Did you find anything on the vehicle following Dakota?" Kieran asked.

"Oh, yeah!" Mitch said. "It parked two blocks from your office. Right in front of the laundry mat. There's a traffic cam across the street. They sat there for about ten minutes before taking off. I ran the license plate and it came back to a rental agency at the airport. I'm still trying to hack into their records to see who rented the car."

"That's them," Kieran stated. "I know it. Where's the vehicle now?"

"I lost them around the Air Force base. The street cams are limited there and I haven't managed to hack into the military ones. But I'm running a program that will alert me if they show back up on the city cams."

"Good job," Kieran praised.

"Okay. I'm going to drive by some of the smaller hotels and motels over here. We'll keep an eye out for the vehicle. Mitch, can you text the license plate and info to both my and Kieran's phones?"

"Sure, I'll send it now."

Kieran turned his attention to the side street that Remy drove down. The neighborhood was rundown but made up of locals. These residents were the heart and blood of the city. It was they who worked twelve-hour shifts inside restaurant kitchens, doing housekeeping, maintenance and more. Without the citizens of Vegas, there wouldn't be fun to have for anyone. Kieran felt a connection with the community. It was why he hunted in their areas. He wanted them to be safe as possible when they were only trying to live their lives.

"Slow down," Kieran murmured. He rolled his window down the rest of the way.

"Did you hear something?" Remy asked.

"Not sure," Kieran said. "Turn into this alley."

Remy didn't even ask questions. He followed directions, but Kieran did see or hear anything as they crawled between fences.

"It must have been nothing," he said. "Go ahead and turn around."

It would be a long night searching this way, but Kieran had faith in their plan.

* * * *

Dakota grinned as Jeremy and Adam told her about their visit earlier with Luca. Apparently, Luca had gone to check on them as soon as he'd arrived and the shifters were in awe of the Coalition agent.

"Did he tell you about his plans?" she asked.

Adam nodded, but she grew concerned when Jeremy dropped his gaze.

"What's wrong?" she asked him.

"I… I'm not sure we should go," Jeremy said.

Adam growled. "We talked about this! We want to go with you."

"But they're coyote shifters!" Jeremy cried. "What if they treat you differently? They might say they want us all, but what if they change their minds?"

"Then you call me and I'll come get you," Dakota answered.

All three teens turned to look at her.

"What?" she asked. "You think just because you're leaving Vegas, you won't see me again?"

"Well…" Carmen responded. "It's not like you even know us."

"Wow!" Dakota shook her head. "I thought we'd bonded over cheeseburgers and fries."

Carmen smiled. "We did!"

Dakota glanced at the boys.

"See," Jeremy said. "Maybe we shouldn't leave."

"Or." Dakota moved to sit next to him on the bed. "You could give this family a chance. I've spent time with Luca. Anyone who raised a guy like that has to pretty awesome. And if you hate it there, all you have to do is call. Kieran and I will be there right away. You'll have our phone numbers and email addresses. We'll keep in touch."

"It would be nice to talk to other shifters, not just coyote, but someone who understands what we're going through," Jeremy said.

"I knew my family," Adam disclosed. "They were great. If my Pack hadn't been killed, they would have taken care of me and you."

"Mine, too," Carmen said. "It's just me and my mom before she died in the car accident, but she was great. It's time you had that."

Dakota couldn't help but beam at these kids. They'd been through so much in their young lives. Every minute that she spent with them, Dakota was awed. The connection between the three was so strong. The teens might be different shifter species, but they'd formed a family. A strong unit to carry on for a lifetime.

"You'll be okay," she promised. "I can just feel it."

"I hope so," Carmen said. "It'd be nice to settle down. Have a bed and clean clothes."

Dakota nodded. She understood the need for a home. Until she'd met and moved in with Kieran, Dakota hadn't known what she'd missed. Now, she couldn't imagine her life going back to how it'd once been.

"Who's hungry?"

They all jumped as Luca entered carrying several pizza boxes.

"Pizza!" Adam exclaimed.

"A kid after my own heart," Luca praised. He handed over the food to Adam. "Hey, Dakota, you're looking better."

"You, too," she replied. "Feeling okay?"

"My leg's a little sore, but nothing too bad."

"You both got hurt?" Jeremy asked. He looked worried.

Dakota patted his leg. "Nothing to be upset about. Just part of the job. Besides, you know how fast shifters heal."

"We'll both be back to one hundred percent in a few days," Luca confirmed. "And I have a question for you three."

"What?" Adam asked, through a mouthful of hot, cheesy, greasy pizza.

"Are you ready for me to break you out of here?"

"Really?" Carmen asked.

"Already?" Jeremy said.

Luca nodded. "I still have a couple things to finish up here. But there's no reason for you all to have to stay. A friend of mine is offering to give us a huge suite for the rest of our stay."

Now things were making sense. "Jackson?" Dakota inquired.

"Yep, and it's nice. Four bedrooms!" Luca said. "And my mate and a couple of friends are already driving down."

"Why?" Jeremy asked. "Why do you need your friends here? Is it because of us?"

"Honestly?" Luca said. "Yes."

Jeremy frowned.

"Now, hear me out." Luca lifted a hand. "My mate is human but has worked with shifters for many years now. Her partner is Cole, a wolf shifter who is one of our team leaders. I thought he could hang out with you some, too. Abilene is another agent with the Coalition. She's a feline shifter and really good friends with my mate, Jade. They want to take all three of you shopping. And I'd feel better if you had agents with you."

"Are we in trouble?" Carmen asked.

"Not at all," Luca said. He nodded toward Dakota. "But we've opened an investigation into the group home that you three ran from. We don't want any other kids, shifter or human, to suffer. That's a big deal and people will be losing their jobs. I just want you safe."

"Your...you...really? You believe us? About how they treated us?" Jeremy asked.

"We believe you," Dakota assured the boy. "And Luca has a point about keeping you safe. Plus you'll get to ask the other shifters tons of questions. That'll be fun."

"And shopping?" Carmen asked.

"Oh, yeah," Luca said. "Jade and Abilene are really looking forward to that part."

Carmen cheered while Adam and Jeremy groaned.

"So what do you say?" Luca questioned.

Both Adam and Carmen looked excited, but Jeremy still appeared scared.

"It's a really nice place," she said. "It's the same hotel that I live in."

"You live in a hotel?" Jeremy asked.

Dakota laughed. "I know, crazy, right? The owner is one of Kieran's best friends and we live together. The room service is awesome and there's a café, buffet and even a couple of stores on the casino level. Although you three have to stay away from the gambling areas."

"It's not like we have any money, anyway," Adam said with a shrug.

"I'll get you some in case you want to go downstairs, but she's serious about the casino. Jackson is really being great about giving us a suite for free. We don't want to get him in trouble."

"No!" Jeremy said. "We wouldn't. We'll behave."

Oh, good. It sounds like Jeremy's getting on board.

"Great!" Luca clapped his hands together. The coyote shifter reminded her so much of Kieran. They both found joy in the smallest things. "Why don't you three finish eating as I wrap things up here? Dakota, you got a minute?"

"Sure." She jumped off the bed. "I'll see you three later." She stole a piece of pepperoni pizza before following Luca out of the room.

He motioned for her to follow him farther down the hall. Dakota quickly ate her piece of pizza as they strolled away from the kids.

"Thanks for backing me in there. I know Jeremy is still unsure," Luca said.

"Well, I believe this is the best for them. Jeremy will come around. Adam and Carmen will help. It's a good idea bringing in a wolf and feline shifter."

"I still have my prisoner to transport. Cole and Abilene are going to take care of that for me so Jade and I can drive the teens to my parents."

"So it's a done deal? Your parents agreed?" She leaned against the wall still a little run down.

"Yep." Luca grinned. "They even got my siblings in on it. They'll get a good old-fashioned Perez family welcome. Everyone is pretty excited."

Dakota blew out a breath then slid down. She stretched her legs out in front of her. Luca knelt beside her.

"You okay?" he asked.

"Yes, this is just such a relief. I don't know what I would have done with them if I hadn't met you."

"I know the Alpha here," Luca said. "He would have taken them in. But his Pack is huge and they might have had trouble fitting in."

"I considered that," she admitted. "Remy would have been there to keep an eye on them, but we work a lot."

"They'll be safe with my family. Can you tell me about the investigation into where they'd been placed?"

"My partners are still working on it. They did make an emergency call and everyone on staff is being held for questioning. A few social workers have been brought in for the time being, but there's a mess. Caspar has assigned them to the case to see it until it ends. I'll join them as soon as the whole fiasco with Kieran's cousins is over."

"Good. If you don't mind getting me their numbers, I would appreciate it. I'd like to keep an eye on the investigation," he stated.

She eyed him suspiciously. "As long as you don't think the Coalition is taking over."

Luca grinned. "Would we do that?"

"Yes!" She threw her hands up. "All the time."

"Hey, I'm not even a team leader. It's not my call. This is personal for me."

"Fine." It wasn't as though Luca couldn't get the numbers another way. Hell, Caspar would probably give it to him if Luca asked. Still, she had to protest, out of pride.

Chapter Nine

It had been two hours without any sign of trouble or his cousins. Kieran grew more agitated as darkness began to fall.

"Remy," Mitch said though the link. "I picked up a nine-one-one call a block from you. The caller states two men attacked a younger guy behind a liquor store."

"On it," Remy said. "Address?"

Kieran straightened in his seat as Mitch rattled off an address. This could be what they needed. If Marcel and Elijah had stopped to feed, their guards might be down. "Jackson?"

"I'm two blocks behind you. I got your back."

Adrenaline coursed through him as the lights from the liquor store appeared. Remy drove carefully to the side of the building. Kieran leapt out before speeding to the back. As the caller had reported, two men had another pinned to the ground. The way the tall, skinny, long-haired, hippy-looking guy was rifling through the poor teenager's pockets, the scene appeared to be a standard assault and burglary.

"Where's your wallet?" Hippy yelled.

"It-it's inside. I don't have any money!" the terrified teen yelled.

Kieran raced down the alley and knocked Hippy Guy off his prey. Hippy grunted when he hit the brick wall.

"Hey!" the hippy's friend, a dirty overweight man, yelled.

Kieran lifted the overweight guy from where he was holding the teen down. Next, Kieran grabbed Fatty's neck.

"K?" Remy called.

"Get this kid inside," Kieran ordered. "Tell the others this is a false call."

"Come on, man." Remy helped the victim off the ground. Now that he wasn't covered by two much bigger bodies, Kieran saw the uniform for the fast food restaurant next to the liquor store.

"I'll meet you back at the truck," Kieran said. He might as well take advantage of the situation. He did need to feed himself.

"Hurry up," Remy called back.

Kieran waited until the back door closed and there were no more witnesses. He brought Fatty's face close to his. Kieran bared his fangs.

"Jesus! Fuck!" Fatty screamed. "What are you?"

"I'm the one who's going to be keeping my eye on you," Kieran threatened. "You and your buddy are going to change your lives around. You will not be taking advantage of anyone ever again."

"Su...sure, man." Fatty nodded.

"See, I don't believe you yet, but by the time I'm through, I'm certain you'll understand."

"Please don't hurt me!"

"Is that what that kid you were holding down said? Did he beg you not to hurt him?"

"Yes! Yes, he did. I'm sorry, man!" Fatty cried.

"Not yet, but you will be," Kieran threatened.

Fatty screamed as Kieran pierced the flesh of his shoulder. He never went for the neck unless he didn't care whether or not he killed his prey. He didn't actually want to end the guy tonight. Things tended to get messy when he took a life and Kieran had other things to do. Kieran took a few long drags before pulling away.

He dropped the man onto the dirty gravel, knowing what was coming next.

Fatty grabbed his stomach, groaning. Kieran sidestepped just as Fatty puked all over himself. Once the guy was done heaving, Kieran knelt down. "Don't forget what I said. I don't want to see around here again."

"Yeah, man," Fatty managed.

Kieran was done there. Hopefully Mitch had called off the emergency call, but if he hadn't, Kieran wasn't in the mood to deal with the local police.

He jogged out of the alley. Remy was already sitting in the truck and had his phone in his hand.

"What's up?" Kieran asked after he climbed back into the passenger seat.

"Mitch picked up that sedan that had been following Dakota. They're about six miles from here."

"Let's go," Kieran ordered.

Remy dropped his cell back on the console before backing the truck from where he'd parked. Kieran was feeling better from the blood and let his head rest of the back of his seat. He loved being warm. One of the temptations Walkers faced was chasing the sensation of a recent feed. Even though Day Walkers only needed to get blood every couple of days, unless they were injured or stressed, some Walkers took blood daily, just to experience the rapture that came with fresh blood.

"It has to be them, right?" Kieran asked his partner.

"If not, we need to see who it is. I don't like the fact that whoever it is has been spotted two days in a row."

"And following Dakota."

Remy grinned.

"The vehicle is on the move. They turned left on Andrews, heading northbound on Grant Street," Mitch broke through,

"Any idea where they're headed?" Kieran asked.

"Looking at a map, there's only houses and bars in the area. They're heading away from the Strip and crowds," Mitch said.

"Hurry up," Kieran ordered Remy. "I don't like this."

Remy pressed harder on the gas pedal. They were speeding through the city, but hopefully, they wouldn't attract the attention of any other law enforcement.

"I got them!" Mitch said excitedly. "You need to get there now! Marcel and Elijah just got out the sedan in front of a bar called the Barn Door."

"Five minutes," Remy said. He gritted his teeth while taking a corner way too fast.

Kieran grabbed the edge of the seat. "Jackson?" he called.

"Right behind you," Jackson replied. "Dakota was already on patrol. She's only a few minutes out, as well. Alex on her tail."

"No!" Kieran yelled. "I don't want her there."

"That's not going to happen," Caspar said. "She's already headed that way."

"Then redirect her!" Kieran shouted. Fuck, he couldn't have her in harm's way once again."

"Come on, K," Remy said. "She wants to get her own revenge on these guys. There are enough of us to take them."

Kieran sighed. "Fine. Tell Alex to watch her back. He's to stay with her the whole time."

"I'll pass it along. You know he'll take care of her," Jackson responded.

"We're pulling up," Remy said.

"They went inside," Mitch said.

Remy pulled in, blocking the dark sedan from being able to back off. If Marcel and Elijah wanted out, they'd have to take out a much bigger truck. Jackson arrived a minute later in his BMW.

"I have other agents on their way," Caspar said. "Be careful."

Kieran opened his door and jumped out. "Jackson, find the back exit and cover it. Remy and I are going in."

Jackson gave him a thumbs-up before jogging off.

Kieran leaned into the truck. "Caspar, have Dakota and Alex stay out front in case Marcel and Elijah get past us."

"Will do," Caspar replied.

Kieran straightened his shirt before looking at Remy. "You ready for this, partner?"

Remy patted his waist where his weapon would be. Kieran had a gun at his ankle but rarely used it. He preferred a more hands-on approach. "Ready."

With long, confident strides, Kieran walked toward the dull red door of the old bar. Not the kind of establishment he'd frequent. He had the feeling that Marcel and Elijah were hunting for their dinner.

He yanked open the door and entered, already running his gaze around the room. Four unknown patrons were seated at the bar, two couples at two different tables, one bartender and his cousins sitting at the closest booth.

Elijah seemed surprised to see him but Marcel just appeared pissed.

He strode across the room, grabbing a chair in his path and slamming it down at the end of the booth.

"Hello, cousins," he greeted.

Marcel growled. "I didn't give you enough credit. Never thought you'd track us down."

Kieran shrugged. "This is what I do."

Marcel glanced past him. "I see the company you keep hasn't improved. Another shifter, really?"

"Yeah." He bared his fangs. "At least I trust them."

"We're your family," Elijah spoke up.

"Who've caused me nothing but trouble since you arrived. So, you want to talk here or after I kick your asses?"

Marcel snorted. "I don't remember you being this cocky. I kind of like it."

"I'm not the same kid you used to double-team. And you don't have Daddy to go whining to. You're in my environment now."

"Whatever, man." Marcel waved his hand. "This city is boring, anyway. There are too many damn shifters."

Kieran had once thought the same thing. He hated the fact he and his cousin had ever agreed on anything. "Why'd you come here?"

"Can we at least get a drink?" Marcel asked.

"Remy," Kieran spoke softly. "Get the bartender and patrons out of the back door."

As soon as Remy started across the bar from his post by the door, Kieran leaned forward. "Looks like they're closing. Why did you come here?"

"Asshole," Marcel muttered.

"That's not right, man," Elijah bitched. "We gotta feed, you know."

"Then you should have stayed home," Kieran sneered. Elijah had always been a little bitch and time had not changed him. "Now, I'm running out of patience."

"How many more agents do you have out there?" Marcel asked.

Kieran just smiled.

"Word has gotten around to the family about you," Marcel said. "We're told you survived ten years at the hands of some shifters."

There was no reason for Kieran to confirm or deny.

"I don't believe it," Elijah said. "Especially seeing as how close you are with those animals."

Kieran shrugged.

"Rumor is you got your revenge on the shifters who'd held you. Took them down through your secret Organization."

He wondered if yawning would be over the top. "Is there a point here?"

"Your father is considering bringing you back into the family," Marcel shared.

It took every bit of his hard-won control for Kieran not to react to Marcel's words. He'd never thought he'd ever hear them. Not that he cared now, but a long time ago, Kieran would have given anything to have won his dad's approval. "And I should care about this?" he quipped.

"You ungrateful little punk," Marcel said with a growl. "Your father, the head of the Argent clan, wants to start training you to take over. I've worked years, doing everything I've been told for that position. I'm not going to let you take it from me."

Kieran laughed. *Holy fuck!* His cousin actually believed that Kieran would accept that offer.

His amusement merely pissed Marcel off more. His cheeks turned red over his pale face.

"So what's the plan? Take me out before my father contacts me?" he guessed.

Marcel flexed his hand.

"You're a fucking idiot," Kieran snarled. "If you'd left me alone, the position would have been yours."

"You say that now," Marcel said. "But you'll eventually want the money, the power. You have no idea how much influence your father has. That you'd have."

"Are you fucking serious?" Kieran snapped. "You do know who I work for? Do you actually believe that we don't know every move my father makes? I probably have more information than you." Sure, he hadn't actually read any of the intel until his cousins had shown up, but they didn't know that.

"Well, it doesn't matter now. Fucking and working with shifters would have been your downfall. Now, we're just saving our family the embarrassment having to learn about your new life. How you've turned your back on what you are."

"Still convinced you can take me?" Kieran asked. He stood and held his arms out to the sides. "Try it."

Marcel didn't need another opening. He attacked quick and viciously. Kieran took a few blows to his face before he got his arm around Marcel's throat. He squeezed hard, but Elijah tackled him to the ground. The three of them went down, but Kieran managed to roll out of the way.

He picked Elijah up before throwing him into a nearby table. Marcel growled then pushed himself up. Kieran leapt at the same time, meeting Marcel in the air. He hit as hard as he could, causing Marcel to grunt, coming down with a pained rumble.

Elijah was slowly getting up, so Kieran rushed over to his side. His bared his fangs and attacked Elijah's neck the same way his cousin had done to Luca. He spat out a good amount of flesh while Elijah screamed.

"No!" Marcel bellowed.

The back door banged open, but Kieran couldn't be concerned with that. Marcel's eyes were glowing, with his fangs in clear view. He was murderous. Well, so was Kieran.

They exchanged blow after blow.

Kieran remained standing, even though Marcel knew how to fight.

He didn't have Kieran's power, though. Kieran's strength was growing instead of him tiring.

"Bastard!" Marcel accused, dropping to his knees. He was realizing that he was no match for Kieran.

"I haven't even started," Kieran responded. He stood over his cousin, staring down at him. "I'll give you one chance to give up."

"Marcel! Don't!" Elijah begged. Jackson had Elijah tied up with a bandage around his neck. "Get out!"

Marcel roared, lunging. He hit Kieran's knees, forcing him down. Kieran's head slammed the wooden floor and bounced. He groaned but swiped at Marcel, catching his legs. Marcel kicked out, landing another strike on his ribs.

"Ugh!" Kieran grunted.

"I'll kill you!" Marcel screamed.

"No, you won't." Dakota stood above both of him with a crowbar in her hand. She brought the weapon down on Marcel's wrist. The crack sounded loudly around them.

Marcel shrieked.

"Finish this, Kieran," Dakota said. "Or I will."

It was time to end this. Kieran turned over onto his knees and just started punching Marcel in the face. He didn't know how many hits he got in before he was yanked away. Jackson spoke softly in his ear, but Kieran still tried to fight him. He wanted to kill his cousin.

"Let it go, K," Jackson murmured. "You're better than him. Let it go."

Kieran threw his head back, roaring to the heavens, before collapsing back into his friend.

The bar was a mess. Broken furniture and blood covered most of the floor.

"Get him in cuffs," Dakota ordered another agent.

Marcel's face looked like hamburger meat, but the Walker was still breathing. "Where's Elijah?" he asked.

"Remy already has him in custody. He'll personally escort him with Alex and Luca."

"Luca's here?" *Damn, how many agents have shown up?*

"Yep, Caspar, too." Jackson loosened his grip. "We tried to help but couldn't get in between the two of you. Guess you had it handled."

Kieran laughed. It felt good.

"Come sit so Dakota can look you over. I think she's about to kick all of us out of here just to be alone with you."

"Yeah, help me sit down."

Jackson led him over to one of booths and he slid in. Dakota was there in an instant.

"Are you hurt?" she asked.

"A little banged up," Kieran admitted. "Nothing too bad."

"I can't believe that you took them both on," she muttered. "I should kick your ass."

"You'd probably win right now."

She snorted. "God, you scared me. And turned me on. I don't know which reaction to be worried about."

Fuck. He chuckled and that really fucking hurt. He was going to have to feed again already. He needed to heal the ribs which hurt the worst. "God! Don't make me laugh."

"You deserve it," she murmured. She was running her fingers gently over his face, neck and shoulders. It appeared that she only needed to touch him. Her aggravation was flowing from her, but the longer her hands were on him, the quicker she calmed.

"It's over," he promised.

Dakota nodded.

"Baby." He caught her wrist before bringing her hand up to his mouth. He brushed his lips across her knuckles. "It's over."

"Okay."

"Where the hell did you get the crowbar?" he asked.

Dakota smiled. "I didn't think you wanted me to shoot your cousin so I had to improvise."

"Well, good job." Kieran peered around the room. Marcel had been taken out and they were alone. "What now?"

"Jackson and Caspar have Marcel. I'm to take you into the office as soon as you're ready. The other agents are going to get this place cleaned up and turned back over to the owner. Caspar said we'd take care of all the damage."

He nodded. That seemed fair.

"Kieran," she said. "What are you going to do about your cousins?"

"Let Caspar prosecute them for whatever he can," Kieran answered.

"And the rest of your family?"

Shit, he was going to have to talk to his father. Even though Kieran didn't want anything to do with the Argent clan, they'd miss Marcel and Elijah eventually. Plus, there was no telling what lies Marcel would say. He'd be able to get a lawyer. With the Argent money, it would be a good one, too. "I'll talk to Caspar. He'll know what to do."

"So, you ready?" she asked.

"Yes! I want to get this over with so I can shower and take you to bed."

Her eyes lit up. "I'm all for that."

* * * *

"You don't have to do this," Caspar advised him.

Kieran sat at his boss's desk with the phone in his hand.

"I can handle this part, as well," Caspar said.

"I have to do it," Kieran said. "I need to close this part of my life."

"I'll leave you alone, then. I think Dakota and Remy are in the hall waiting for you to finish. Once you're done here, go on home. We can finish the rest of the paperwork tomorrow. We'll let your cousins sit in the medical wing and stew."

"They're under guard?"

"I've got it covered," Caspar replied.

"Okay. Give me a minute to get this done."

Caspar grasped his shoulder hard for a long moment before he strolled out of the office. Kieran was now alone, having to call a number he'd sworn he'd never dial. He took a deep breath then punched in the numbers.

"Argent residence."

"I need to speak with Elder Argent. This is Agent Smith from the Organization," he said calmly. He wondered if it was the same housekeeper from his childhood. Veronica had been kind to him, but Kieran didn't remember her voice so he didn't say anything else to her.

"Please hold." He didn't know why he expected music on the other end of the line. Instead Kieran just heard silence. Long minutes went by before he heard the voice.

"This is Elder Argent."

Kieran had to close his eyes. His father's voice. He never thought he'd hear that sound again.

"Hello?" his father barked.

"It's Kieran," he said.

There was a moment of pause. "Son?"

"Yes." Kieran swallowed. "I'm calling you with some news."

"Go ahead."

There were no questions on how he'd been. His dad probably didn't care.

"Marcel and Elijah have been arrested and are in the custody of the Organization. They'll be processed in the morning so you should expect a phone call."

"I take it they are in Las Vegas with you."

So, his dad did know where he lived. "Yes." Kieran didn't know what else to say. A small part of him just wanted to hang up. He should have let Caspar call. But he was a man and he needed to face his fears.

His dad sighed. "I suspected as much. I'll give their father a call and let him know."

"You don't sound surprised," Kieran commented.

"As I said, I suspected that was where they'd gone. My brother informed me they were out of town. I didn't ask questions. It's a logical assumption they'd go after you."

"Well, they failed."

"That's obvious, as it is you ringing me."

"And have been arrested."

"You already said that. There is no need to repeat yourself."

"You don't care?" Kieran asked. *Is there no love in my family at all?*

"If they were stupid enough to fail and get caught then they must suffer the consequences. It is no matter to me."

Fuck, Kieran came from this man. If his life hadn't been detoured at eighteen, he might have been exactly like him. "Okay… Well…I just wanted you to hear the news about Marcel and Elijah from me. I guess I'll let you go."

"You don't have anything else to say or ask?" His father sounded disappointed.

Kieran huffed. "What do you want me to say, Dad?"

"How about asking about your mother or sisters?"

Guilt tore at him. "Why?" He channeled his anger. "Have they asked about me? Ever wondered what happened to me?"

His father's silence was enough of an answer.

"That's what I thought," Kieran said.

"What about asking to come home?"

"Why would I do that?" Kieran inquired. "You sent me away. Told me that I needed to become a man."

"And from the reports that I'm getting, you have. It's time for you to return to your family."

"Family?" Rage consumed him. "I have my family here. I don't need you."

"The humans and shifters?" His father scoffed. "You're an Argent. It's time for you to stop playing around and take on your responsibilities."

"I'm not playing around. I have a job that I'm good at. I'm in love. I have friends who'd do anything for me. I don't need you."

"You will. What's going to happen when your humans die of old age? Or when your lover falls for one of her own kind? I know all about the people you surround yourself with. The only one I approve of is Jackson Wickham. He'll be a good contact for the family."

"Listen carefully," Kieran demanded. "Stay away from my friends and me. Do not try to contact me. Just leave us alone."

"You don't understand, Kieran. This isn't a choice you can make. You will fulfill your destiny."

"My destiny?" he spat. "Are you fucking kidding me? I'm done with you. With the entire family. I'm sorry I even called."

"But you did. Because you have obligations to us. I'll give you two weeks to return. At that time, you'll take your place at my side."

"Not going to happen," Kieran responded.

"And, Kieran, I disapprove of coarse language. That is something you'll have to curb. It's unbecoming."

"I don't give a shit what you approve of," Kieran taunted.

"Two weeks, Kieran. Or I'll retrieve you myself and you don't want that." His father hung up. He actually hung up on Kieran.

Kieran roared before throwing the phone across the room.

The door cracked open. Kieran whirled around. Dakota leaned through the opening. "All done?" she asked brightly.

Kieran stared at her.

She sighed then entered, closing the door behind her. "Didn't go well?"

"That bastard actually thinks that I'll go home to him."

"Really?" Dakota seemed surprised. "Even though you surround yourself with shifters? I though Marcel was going to tattle on you. Isn't that what he said?"

"Apparently, my father is already aware of who I spend my time with. He informed me it was time for me to take care of my responsibilities to the family."

"Screw him," she said. "You don't have to do anything you don't want to." Dakota strolled across the room, smiling. "You're an adult."

"I know… It's just…"

"Do you want to go home?" She'd stopped walking. The expression on her face broke her heart. "It's… If you want…"

He shook his head. Kieran didn't know how to explain how he felt. What if his father was right? Caspar, Dean and the other humans would die of old age. A person had to be born a Day Walker or shifter. There was no getting scratched or bitten to turn into a paranormal. Even though Kieran didn't like to think about it, the truth of the matter was that Caspar would die eventually.

"Kieran?" Dakota asked.

And Dakota—would she find another jaguar or feline? Was there a shifter she was meant to be with? Could Kieran be standing in the way of her happiness? Maybe he should leave Vegas, letting her get on with the rest of her life.

"No! You know what? Just no." She stomped over to him and grabbed the front of his shirt. "I'm not going to let you push me away because of something that asshole said."

"And if he's right?" Kieran murmured.

"Fuck that! And fuck you if you think for a minute of leaving me or any of us." She was pissed off. Kieran had seen her angry numerous times, but never to this level.

"Just give me a minute to think."

"Nope." Dakota tugged him forward. "You're doing too much of that at the moment. You need to feel." She kissed him. Hard and demanding.

Kieran held back a moan of pleasure. He loved the feel of her soft yet strong body pressed up against his. If he had a weakness, it was Dakota. His father would use that against him. Even if he didn't want to leave, Kieran was going to have to think about how his decisions would affect her.

Dakota drew back. "Turn your mind off."

"I can't help it," he confessed. "I don't know what to do."

She pushed away from him. "Then we'll figure it out." Dakota walked over to the couch then plopped down. "Break it down for me." She patted the cushion beside her. Kieran gingerly joined her.

Kieran pressed his lips together. He didn't know where to begin.

"Don't think about what you're saying," she advised. "Just spit it out."

"If I don't go home, my father will come from me. He told me that and I believe him. He'll also hurt anyone who gets in his way."

"So, your dad is going to come all the way to Las Vegas to drag you home? Instead of fighting him, you could just fall in line and be a good son. That's option one," she said.

"Option two?" he asked.

"You make him come here. If he wants you that badly, then he'll need to fetch you himself. After that, you show him, prove to him, that you're your own man. You won't be joining him or returning to Texas."

"And if he tries to make me?" Kieran questioned.

"You are the strongest, most powerful Walker in existence. Even at this moment, you don't even know everything you can do. It's your choice whether you find that out here or with people you know you can't trust."

"How do you make it sound so simple?"

Dakota laughed. "I'm not saying anything you don't know. Your dad managed to fuck with your head. He put doubt in your mind. From what I've read, he is a master manipulator."

"You think he's manipulating me?"

"I do," she said. "The question is, don't you?"

"Yes," he admitted.

"So?"

"He didn't lie, though. Caspar and the other humans are going to die on me. It might be years from now, but eventually it won't matter how strong I am. The humans, my humans, will die."

"I know," she murmured. "It's not going to hurt any less now than in the future, though. Why not treasure the time you have with Caspar while you can? Besides, if you're not around, how will you know Caspar is taking care of himself?"

Kieran grinned. "Playing on my sympathies. Good one."

"I thought so. Now, let's move on to me. What did your dad say about me? That I'll betray you? Maybe turn you over to another group of shifters?" She held up a finger. "No, I got it. I'll find a jaguar or shifter and fall in love with him. I'll leave you for someone of my own kind."

He jerked back.

"Yeah, I should have guessed that one right away."

"We don't know what's in store for us. Our future," he pointed out.

"We don't," she agreed. Dakota lifted up before swinging her leg over him to straddle his waist. "No one does. But I love you. And I know you love me, too. I'm not worried about the future. It will take care of itself."

"Why haven't you ever brought up mating?" It was a question he both often wondered about and avoided. Kieran didn't want to pressure her, but they were laying all their cards on the table. This was the biggest moment of their relationship.

Dakota stiffened. Yes, that was the reaction he'd expected.

"You don't have to answer."

She shook her head. "Are you sure you want to have this conversation?"

"I think we have to."

"Fine." Dakota cupped his face, lifting it so she peered into his eyes. "I want to mate with you. I have for a very long time. But I know you're not ready for that kind of commitment."

"I'm not afraid of commitment," he argued.

"No," she said. "But you're not open to shifter rituals, either. You might run with my jaguar, but sometimes you still shy away. I don't need to mate with you. I just want to."

"But you've never said anything to me."

She nodded. "Maybe I should have. I just don't want you to push me away."

"If I turn my father down, we're going to have to be very careful. There can't be any secrets between us."

"If?" she repeated. "Kieran, we both know you're not going to go back to a family that deserted you. You're too loyal."

"Then why are we having this conversation?" he asked.

"Because it's time." She leaned forward to brush her lips against his. "Communication is key."

Kieran laughed. "I do love you."

"I know."

"And we should talk more about mating. Maybe just not at this moment."

Dakota rocked against him. "What should we be doing instead?"

"How long do you think we have until Remy or Caspar break in?"

"I locked the door," Dakota said.

"Like that would stop them."

"So we'd better hurry," she teased. Dakota grabbed the hem of her shirt before tugging it over her head.

Kieran bent, kissing her lush breasts trapped behind her sports bra. Soft and perfect, just like every inch of her.

"I want you to fuck me over Caspar's desk."

He groaned. He was all for that. Kieran stood, keeping his hold on her, then strolled across the room. He laid her back onto the cool wood surface before he took a step to the side.

She grinned as he unsnapped her jeans. "Hurry." She slapped his hand away. "Get your pants down."

Kieran moved his hands to his waist as Dakota finished undressing. This was crazy and wild. They really shouldn't be having sex in the boss's office.

Dakota kicked off her boots before removing her socks, pants and panties. She sat up long enough to remove her bra. Kieran undressed quickly until he was completely naked. He was already hard.

"You are so beautiful," he murmured.

She ran her hands over her breasts then down her stomach.

Kieran inched closer. He licked his lips, craving a taste of her sweet juices.

"Put your hands on me!" she ordered.

He grinned. Kieran wrapped his hands around her waist to yank her forward. Then he lowered his mouth to her legs. Kieran spread her thighs, breathing in her sweet flavor.

"Don't tease."

Kieran licked right between the folds of her pussy.

"Yes!"

"I'm not teasing now, am I?"

"K!"

Chuckling, he went back to enjoying her. He used his tongue, fingers and lips to bring her pleasure. Dakota shuddered and moaned. Fuck, he could get off just on the sounds she was making.

"God!" she yelled and climaxed.

Kieran continued to pump his fingers into her while sucking on her clit until she collapsed back onto the desk. "My turn." He climbed up onto the furniture with her. Dakota pushed herself higher up to make room.

He pushed the tip of his cock inside, but she put her hand on his chest. Kieran paused.

"Look at me, in my eyes. We might not be fully mated, but I am yours, Kieran."

"Yes." He pressed forward. Her inner muscles clamped down on his shaft, tight and hot. The heat spread from his cock through his entire body. A feeling of peace swamped over him.

Dakota lifted her hips, forcing him in deeper.

Kieran pumped his hips in an effort to finally slide all the way inside her. It was difficult to keep his eyes open, but Kieran managed it. He gazed down at her beautiful face. He'd been an idiot earlier. There was no way Kieran would give Dakota or their life together up.

She was who he was meant to be with. Dakota belonged to Kieran and him to her. It might not last — who knew — but he would enjoy every single second he had with her. At least, she had put up a fight for him. The way she'd always said she would.

"More," Dakota demanded.

Kieran braced his knees before raising her hips higher to plunge deep and fast. She arched while throwing her hands out, knocking over pens and paper. Kieran growled as he thrust. He could feel the tingle at the base of his spine signaling his release.

"Come inside me," she said.

He slammed forward and released. Kieran kept pumping his hips until she began bucking against him. A dozen strokes later, Dakota threw her head back, orgasming. Kieran fell forward.

Someone pounded on the door. "You done yet? I can't keep Caspar away any longer."

Kieran banged his head on the desk. "Sometimes I hate my partner."

Dakota laughed. "He did cover for us. I think we owe him."

"Hey!" Remy shouted as he beat on the door again. "Luca said you're already late for dinner!"

"Shit, I forgot about that," Dakota muttered.

"About what?" Kieran lifted his head. They were both sweaty and covered in fluids. And she'd never looked better.

"Don't be mad."

"I don't like where this is going," he complained.

"So Jackson got Luca and the three teens a suite in our hotel."

"Okay."

"And Luca's mate and two other Coalition agents are here. I said we'd join them for dinner." She spoke quickly.

"You did what?"

"In my defense, it was before you took down your cousins and had a reunion of sorts with your dad," she teased. "We could cancel, but they're headed out in the morning. The kids would like to see you to say goodbye."

Kieran groaned. "Fine." They re-dressed hurriedly. "We're cleaning up first, though."

"Yes, dear," Dakota quipped.

His phone rang. Kieran groaned, reaching for it. "What now?" There was no way his father had gotten his personal cell phone number already. He expected his dad to have the ability, but this was too much at the moment. Hell, his father wouldn't care. Plus he'd known where Kieran was so maybe he did already have Kieran's number.

Relief flooded him when he saw the Alpha's name on his display.

"Yes?" he snapped.

"I'll forgive the rudeness once again," Damon stated. "But we must work on your manners."

Kieran found himself grinning. "I only do it to annoy you, anyway."

"I'm aware." Damon didn't sound amused.

"Did you need something? Or are you just calling to say hi?"

"I'm calling," Damon stressed, "to let you know I won't hold you to your promise that I get my chance at the two Walkers who attacked my Pack."

Shit, he'd forgotten about that. "Oh...I..."

"Remy informed me that you put a pretty good beating on your cousins. Since they're your family, I'll let it go."

"They're not my family," Kieran almost shouted.

Damon chuckled. "That's right. They are not. I actually like the people you consider your family."

He glanced over to where Dakota was smiling at him. Of course, she could hear both sides of the conversation. The worry he'd seen in her gaze earlier was gone. He'd done something to please her.

"I've made you speechless," Damon said. "I think I like you better silent."

"Very funny," Kieran responded. "But, yeah, I did show my cousins not to fuck with us. There might…be other Walkers coming. I'm not sure how the rest of my family is going to take Marcel's and Elijah's arrests."

"We'll be ready," Damon said. "I'll admit that I let my guard down. I'm used to dealing with Jackson and his Walkers. You need to remember that you're not alone. If you need anything from me or my Pack, just let me know."

Kieran still didn't like the Alpha, but they had come to some sort of friendship. "Thanks. I appreciate it."

"No problem. Oh, Max went by to see Alex before Alex went to help you. Said they spoke."

"Alex seems to be okay," Kieran said. "Whatever happened must have helped."

"Max said it helped him, as well. They've set up a weekly dinner."

Kieran was relieved. "Good."

"So I'll talk to you later. Bring your girl out sometime to run. I think she'd like to check out more of the caves, this time without the threat of crazy shifters."

Dakota was already nodding.

"She'd like that. I'll talk to you later." He hung up, avoiding looking back at Dakota. He had too many damn people in his life. And he couldn't even bitch about it since it was his doing.

Chapter Ten

The sound inside the suite was loud. Kieran grimaced as he and Dakota stood outside the door. He was freshly showered and changed but tired. He didn't really want to do this, but he did want to see the teens before they left.

"It won't be that bad," Dakota said. She knocked on the door, grinning. "Just give them an hour."

"They're here!" He heard Carmen shout.

"Calm down and let me get the door. Turn that music down, too. They've had a long night," Luca called.

Dakota glanced at him. "Oh, come on! This will be fun. You need more fun in your life."

"I have fun," he argued. She snorted in response. "I do!"

The door opened. Luca stood there was a big smile on his face. "Thanks for coming. I know it's a lot to ask, but the kids really wanted to see you."

"We don't mind," Dakota replied.

"Well, come in. Jackson sent up some room service. There's plenty for everyone. Some of the food's not bad. As long as you get past the corndogs, pizza pockets, cheese sticks and cake."

"I love cheese sticks." Kieran pushed his way past. Not only was he hungry for food, but he'd have to get blood soon, too. In the meantime, he really did love cheese sticks.

"We have five kinds of dipping sauce." Adam pointed to a tray. "I don't know what that pink stuff is, but the other ones are good."

"Horseradish," a tall man beside Adam stated. He smelt of shifter, wolf, and eyed Kieran warily.

Kieran dipped his head before stealing a stick from Adam. He shoved it into his mouth.

"He's an adult," Dakota said behind him. "I swear."

Kieran merely grinned before grabbing more food.

"Let me introduce you around," Luca said. "Cole is one of the team leaders at the Coalition." He pointed. "Sitting there is Abilene, a pretty badass agent. She also puts up with one of the absolute craziest tiger shifters I've ever met." Abilene flipped him off before going back to eating a salad that didn't look appealing at all.

"And this" — Luca held out a hand — "is the love of my life. My mate, Jade."

"Hello." Jade waved. "Thanks for getting Luca stabbed in the leg and a chunk taken out of him."

"He healed," Kieran quipped.

Jade laughed. "Yes, he did. But now he'll be absolutely insufferable, going on and on about taking on a Walker."

Kieran shrugged. "He actually did a good job."

Jade frowned. "Please don't encourage him."

"I'm Kieran and I'm hungry," he said. "That's Dakota. Don't fuck with her and we'll all get along well."

"Language." Dakota smacked the back of his head.

"It's not like they haven't heard bad words before," Kieran griped.

"They need good influences. No more running around on the streets. From here on out, they'll act their ages," Luca said. He glared at the teens. "Isn't that right?"

"Yes," Jeremy and Carmen said together. Adam squinted at him.

"Right, Adam?" Luca stressed.

"Yeah, sure."

No one believed Adam for a second. It was almost funny. Kieran bent so he was eye to eye with the teen. "Don't think you can pull anything over on these guys. They're trained agents. If you get into trouble, I'm going to drive down and kick your ass."

Adam swallowed hard. "O…okay. I'll behave."

"Good." Kieran nodded. "Now, where's the booze? I deserve a drink."

"Dakota! Let me show you the new clothes I got today." Carmen tugged on her hand.

Kieran was glad he didn't have to go look at clothes. Instead he sat between Adam and Jeremy. Cole was smiling then took a seat across from Kieran.

"You're going to have to tell us the real story of how Luca attacked the Walker. I don't believe a word he says," Cole said.

"Hey! Fuck you, man," Luca groused.

"Language!" Dakota and Jade yelled.

"Okay." Kieran started to pile a plate with more food. He didn't worry about healthy choices, though. He chose the same stuff that the boys did. "So I'm facing off with my cousins. Both are real bad dudes. But Marcel always liked to pretend to be in charge. So he's there running his mouth with Luca sneaking up behind him and Elijah." He didn't plan to tell the entire story and he had to keep it PG rated, but he could see the excitement on Adam's and Jeremy's faces.

"I was like a ninja," Luca said.

Cole snorted. "Yeah, right, man. I've fought beside you. You'd trip over your own feet."

"I'm a machine," Luca argued. "I could take them on again."

"Anyway," Kieran said loudly. "I'm keeping Marcel busy as Elijah is cowering behind him. Luca launches himself at Elijah."

"It was badass!" Luca whispered. Probably so he wouldn't get in trouble again.

"As Luca strikes, I go after Marcel. There I am battling my older cousin and I hear a roar. It was terrifying."

"Because I'm a badass!" Luca repeated.

"Luca!" Jade yelled.

"Badass," Luca murmured.

"Who's been tamed by a wee little human," Cole taunted.

"You want to talk about who's been neutered, wolf? How about I get your mate on the phone, Alpha?" Luca responded.

"You're an Alpha?" Adam asked.

Cole nodded.

"But we're telling my story," Luca said. "Cole can tell you later how he was given one of the largest Packs in the state."

Kieran laughed. He'd never thought he'd joke around with shifters like this. Fuck, he was actually surrounded by them, with only one human in the mix.

Six weeks ago this would have been impossible.

Ever since he'd taken down the ones responsible for his years of torment, Kieran had been working up to this moment.

Acceptance.

He'd found it not only in himself but those around him. Caspar had told him to embrace his powers, who he was. Kieran was doing more than that, though.

He was embracing his life.

The one that he had. The one that he would have.

Kieran was a monster. He was a hero. A lover, friend, agent and so much more.

* * * *

Dakota held on to Kieran's hand until he'd closed the bedroom door behind them. It had been a long night — shit, it had been a long few days. But the worst was behind them.

In a few hours, the Organization would be prosecuting Marcel and Elijah. They'd have a lawyer. Even be given the opportunity to defend themselves. However, Dakota was certain that Caspar would make sure they paid for all their sins.

The three teens had a home, finally. Luca would be leaving later that day to take the three shifters to his parents' home. She couldn't think of a better ending for them.

"Why're you so quiet?" Kieran asked.

He was slowly undressing, looking exhausted.

So maybe not everything was settled. She knew that they would be facing Kieran's father sooner rather than later. But, at least they'd do so together, with the help of their friends. It wouldn't be easy—the Argent clan had a lot of power. Kieran had love, though. It sounded cliché and overly romantic, yet Dakota had faith.

"Dakota, you okay?"

"Yeah, just tired, I guess."

Kieran dropped his shirt on the floor where his boots and socks already were. "Just think. If we didn't deserve a vacation before, we do now."

"That's a good point." She began to strip while walking to her own side of the bed. "So, beach or mountains?"

"Anywhere other than Texas is fine by me."

Dakota laughed. "Yeah. I hear it's hot there."

"I could take you to Paris," Kieran said. "Wouldn't that be romantic?"

She pulled back the blankets. "Come on. Climb in." Kieran slid onto the cool sheets before putting his arm around her. She flipped the covers over them. Dakota snuggled into his chest. "We could just stay in the suite. Not answer the door or phones," she suggested.

"That would fine for a couple of days. The more I think about it, though, the more I really want to take you somewhere. Away from the city and all of our responsibilities."

"Maybe for a week or two, that would be nice. But then we'll come home."

He brushed his lips over her forehead. Dakota felt treasured, lying with him like that. Kieran might be a badass Walker, probably one of the most powerful paranormals in the world, but he was also so gentle with her.

"I can't believe this is where I feel at home. I hate this city."

"You *hated* it," she corrected. "We both know that it's grown on you. That's why you hunt where the locals are — to protect them. You could use Jackson's feeders or some tourist downstairs. Instead, you go out of your way to take care of the residents."

"If I have to live here, I might as well take care of the people who are trying to just make a living," Kieran said.

"Well, I'm up for reassignment in a couple of months. I guess we could see about moving," she said.

Kieran stiffened. "What? Why didn't you tell me?"

Dakota laughed. "I already requested to stay. Caspar approved the paperwork as soon as he took over."

"That wasn't funny," Kieran bitched. "We just bought this place."

"I just wanted to check that you haven't changed your mind." That and she enjoyed messing with him.

Kieran rolled her over until she was on her back with him leaning over her. "You're becoming such a smartass."

"You must be rubbing off on me."

"Oh, I'll rub off on you all right." He kissed her while he did indeed start to rub his hardening erection against her leg.

"I hope you'll do more than that."

Kieran laughed. "If I wasn't so tired, I'd show you what I can do many times. Instead, I'll just have to love you long and slow tonight."

Dakota threw her arms around his neck. "Show me."

"Maybe I have more energy than I thought." Kieran sat up to position himself between her legs.

"You always do," she said. Dakota closed her eyes to enjoy the feel of his tongue over her collarbone and lower. She gave herself to her lover. Kieran would always be there to take care of her.

About the Author

Crissy Smith lives in Texas with her husband, daughter, and three Labrador retrievers. The three dogs love to curl up under her computer desk and nap while she writes. It doesn't leave a lot of room for her but what's a woman to do?

When not writing or reading, she enjoys hunting, camping and shooting. But she has a girly side too and is addicted to pedicures and coffee.

She has been writing since she was a teenager and still loves everything to do with the paranormal. Her stories and characters all have a place in her heart. She loves the Alpha male, the dominant werewolf, and the Master vampire, which find their way in most of her books.

Learn more about the characters she has created at her website where they have their very own page. It will be updated from time to time to let you know what's going on with them. Also you can find out who will be in the next book.

Crissy loves to hear from readers. You can find her contact information, website details and author profile page at http://www.totallybound.com.